THE UNSAID

AARON BLAYLOCK

THE UNSAID

AARON BLAYLOCK

BONNEVILLE
BOOKS

An Imprint of Cedar Fort, Inc.
Springville, Utah

This is a work of fiction. The characters, names, incidents, places, and dialogue are products of the author's imagination and are not to be construed as real. The opinions and views expressed herein belong solely to the author and do not necessarily represent the opinions or views of Cedar Fort, Inc. Permission for the use of sources, graphics, and photos is also solely the responsibility of the author.

ISBN 13: 978-1-4621-1905-9

Published by Bonneville Books, an imprint of Cedar Fort, Inc.
2373 W. 700 S., Springville, UT 84663
Distributed by Cedar Fort, Inc., www.cedarfort.com

LIBRARY OF CONGRESS CATALOGING-IN-PUBLICATION DATA

Names: Blaylock, Aaron, 1977- author.
Title: The unsaid / Aaron Blaylock.
Description: Springville, Utah : Bonneville Books, an imprint of Cedar Fort, Inc., [2016]
Identifiers: LCCN 2016028922 (print) | LCCN 2016037661 (ebook) | ISBN 9781462119059 (softcover : acid-free paper) | ISBN 9781462126842 (epub, pdf, mobi)
Subjects: | GSAFD: Christian fiction. | Love stories.
Classification: LCC PS3602.L3995 U57 2016 (print) | LCC PS3602.L3995 (ebook) | DDC 813/.6--dc23
LC record available at https://lccn.loc.gov/2016028922

Cover design by Michelle May Ledezma
Cover design © 2016 by Cedar Fort, Inc.
Edited and typeset by Jessica Romrell

Printed in the United States of America

10 9 8 7 6 5 4 3 2 1

Printed on acid-free paper

To my beautiful, courageous wife. You are the voice in my head, in a good way. You make me want to be good and do good. Thank you for not giving up on me. I love you, La.

DOTAR

Why does one leave a thought unspoken? Is it because it is deemed of little consequence? Perhaps it seems unnecessary or unimportant. It can be out of fear or as a kindness, but in most cases, it is because there is simply not enough time.

Time, however, was not something Maggie concerned herself with. Time, after all, was measured by man. And while she was certainly aware of time, it was not hers she kept. Her clock had not yet begun to tick. For that she must wait and watch as his time rolled on.

"Maggie," a soft voice next to her called. "What are you doing over there?"

Maggie turned her attention from the glow of the screen in front of her to the voice beside her. There she found the pleasant image of her friend Vila. The sea of figures in the distance moved in and out of focus as they passed behind her translucent face. A majestic smile projected from her and touched Maggie's soul.

"She is studying the finites again," Borador said. He stood next to Vila. "What else would she be doing?"

"Leave her be," the soft-spoken Vila rebuked. "Is that so, Maggie?"

"That is so," Maggie replied.

Maggie loved to study the words and deeds of humanity. She spent much of her free time absorbed in the text displayed on her monitor and marveled at their insight, despite their incomplete knowledge and limited perceptive. She found their search for understanding and meaning to be a thing of beauty and longed to join with them.

"And what is it that has you pondering?" Vila asked.

"Love recognizes no barriers. It jumps hurdles, leaps fences, penetrates walls to arrive at its destination full of hope," Maggie answered.

"That is beautiful," said Vila. "Who spoke it?"

"Maya Angelou," Maggie replied. "She is a poet."

Vila's countenance grew brighter as she and Maggie regarded each other. Hurdles, fences, and walls were things of the physical world—things she had yet to experience. Notwithstanding the fact that she did not know what it was to jump, leap, or penetrate, she loved the imagery. In her limited prism of their world she had seen such barriers and witnessed such acts but could only imagine what it felt like. Love and hope on the other hand were emotions she was well acquainted with. Love was what bore her into existence and hope had guided her to where she was.

The only barriers in her world were artificial ones, barriers of light and energy designed to emulate the physical world; however, for beings of light and energy themselves, these were not really barriers at all. Still, most respected these walls since it was good practice for the life to come.

The four walls that surrounded them rose out and up into the heavenly cosmos. An infinite array of stars pulsed amid a dark universal ocean. Beneath them was a bright sheet of white light that simulated a floor. Within the room were countless spirits mingling amongst oval shaped energy platforms, which hovered in front of them like tables. This place of gathering was called the congreget. Everything in the congreget, including the walls, the floor, and the platforms, was a brilliant white, but nothing shone as bright as the spirits who occupied the faux room.

"But why do you study at all?" a young spirit next to Vila named Dae asked. "I mean, when your turn comes, you will not remember any of this."

"That is what I say," said Borador. "Seems like a waste to me."

"You mean like quren?" Vila shot back.

Quren was a game played by many in the space between their labors. A ball of light was pushed back and forth across the top of the oval energy platforms by a small beam of light that was confined to the perimeter. The ball moved at an ever-increasing rate until the player failed to contain it. Borador hovered over the platform nearest him with a ball of light bouncing frantically around the inside of the oval while he maneuvered the beam quickly to corral it.

"This is sharpening my reflexes," Borador contended. "There is nothing which states those will not carry over."

Borador was an intimidating presence. He had strong opinions about every topic and never failed to share them. His spirit was old and immense. It was not his stature alone that made him stand out; it was the intensity of his gaze, which somehow seemed to magnify his enormous frame. He did not look up from his game but his vexation was felt by all.

"Nothing says our knowledge will vanish as we pass through," Maggie said, unwilling to back down. "Our memories, yes, but I believe that knowledge will endure. Down there, the lessons we learn will be from mortality, but truth and knowledge are eternal. Down there, they are to be remembered, not acquired."

"Well said, my dear," said Vila.

Borador continued to play his game and grumbled, "A lot of wisdom from a tyro."

"Borador, that is not fair," Vila exclaimed.

"Fair or not, it is true," he rebutted. "She has not seen half the things I have. If she had, she would not bother with the finites and what they think they know. They wander, they hurt, they suffer, and they cause those around them to suffer. They do not see, they only think they see."

With his attention off of his game, the ball of light burst free from the platform and shot through the wall at the far end of the room. It passed through a group of startled spirits who fell silent and looked to the spot where the ball had absorbed into the wall.

The light around Borador increased in volume but not in brightness. After a few moments his countenance returned to normal. Two spirits nearest him exited the room swiftly, whether out of necessity or flight one could not be sure.

"Forget it," Borador said, and he floated out through the exit.

Those in the room returned to their normal subdued conversations after the momentary excitement passed. There was a steady flow of activity as spirits entered and exited the ever-changing room. Maggie looked to the last spot she had seen Borador and considered following after him.

"Let him go," Vila counseled. "It is out and gone."

"What was that about?" Dae asked.

"This is Borador's third time through DOTAR," Vila explained. "He has forfeited his spot twice now and had to begin all over again."

"Why would he do that?" Dae asked.

"He will not talk about it," Vila said. "But there are those unfortunates who go down into unspeakable tragedy and some lose themselves on the other side. When your beholden is a wayward it can be difficult to witness the things they do and often their thoughts are far worse. Some curators cannot take the darkness and withdraw rather than endure."

Maggie felt sorry for Borador and really anyone with the misfortune of being assigned to a wayward. As a curator, their task was to record only the unspoken thoughts of their beholden. They were, of course, privy to all their words and deeds but those things were written in the Book of Life, a physical log kept by The Department of Acts and Records. However, since every act begins with a thought, it was their job to collect and catalog thoughts until they became acts. A curator was bonded to their beholden until the end of their life. The process of thought collection required intense connection during every waking moment of their beholden's day. Such a connection was difficult for beings of light, especially when subjected to the darkness of a wayward. Difficult or not, a successful tour in the Department of Thoughts and Records was a requirement of every spirit before their own mortal journey.

"Will he be okay?" Dae asked.

"Of course," Vila assured her. "Much has been asked of him and his burden is great, but that is because he is strong."

Maggie was not so sure. Of his strength of spirit she had no doubt, but the toll of all he had experienced had changed him. Light is more powerful than darkness but prolonged exposure to darkness can dim even a powerful light.

"Come, my dear," Vila said to Dae. "She is waking."

Being new to DOTAR, Dae had not yet been assigned her own beholden and was paired with Vila to observe and learn the job of a curator. With her beholden near the end of her life, Vila was as experienced as a curator could get. Dae loved and appreciated her mentor but was full of questions and enthusiasm; just one of the reasons Maggie enjoyed her presence.

"Until our next, Maggie," Dae said.

"Until then," Maggie replied.

Dae and Vila exited through the same opening as Borador with their robes flowing behind them. Like the department itself, their spirits took a form and shape that mirrored their future temporal state. They were ethereal copies of the temporal bodies they hoped to join with soon. Everything was in its proper place from their head down to their toes. Glorious white robes of light covered their spirit bodies and hung just above their feet.

Despite the activity in the congreget, there was a sweet and undisturbed calm as everyone conducted themselves with a reverence for the work they performed. Maggie took in the peace from the atmosphere and allowed it to fill her being. In the calm, she felt a stirring inside her—a tug, which she imagined was close to what a physical feeling must be like. Her beholden was about to awake and she could feel it. Soon she would be engaged in his every thought. Without hesitation she followed the course her friends had taken out of their congreget and into a long hallway. Thousands of tiny beams of light shot down the hall like threads in a tapestry. She crossed to the other side of the pulsing hallway and the bright white wall of light parted in front of her. She passed over the threshold and the wall formed again behind her.

The room she entered, the box as it was commonly known, was much smaller than the congreget. Similar to the rest of the department, the box had four walls and a floor but there was a ceiling just overhead so as to shut out any external influences. Besides Maggie and a small oval platform near the center of the room, the box was empty. She enjoyed the solitude of the box, but with him she was not truly alone. As she approached the platform, it energized and lit up. A light blue vertical slit formed on the wall in front of her and spread from top to bottom. The tear in the wall expanded into an oval identical to the platform, only five times the size. Within the blue-bordered oval was a scene of a shabby but well-kept bedroom. Daylight seeped through venetian blinds and made a ladder-like pattern on the carpeted floor. The red numbers on the digital display on the nightstand read 7:00. A colorful blue, yellow, white, and black bedspread adorned with his favorite Star Wars characters, was pulled up over a lump in the center of a twin bed next to the window. The lump twisted and moved side to side and then all at once a young man threw off the covers and slid his legs off the side of the bed. *Morning. Too early. Ugh.*

His sandy brown hair stuck straight up like a rooster's comb. With one hand he wiped across his face and picked a tiny fleck of crust from his eye. *Eye goober.* He sat silently with his head hung and stared at the floor.

Cold, so cold. Eh. I don't want this. Maybe I'll call in. No, I should go. What's today? Tuesday? You can't call in on a Tuesday. Get up.

Maggie worked frantically as the platform in front of her sprang to life. His thoughts echoed into the box and clear blue text appeared within the large oval portal on the wall, paired with duplicate text on the platform directly in front of her. She captured each thought and shifted it to the appropriate repository. With each cataloged thought a thread of light streamed from the platform and ran up the wall and out of the box.

Alarm. A cock-a-doodle-doo emanated from the alarm clock next to his bed, which now read 7:01. *Shut it, rooster.* He reached over and tapped the snooze bar on top of the clock. *Take that.* He opened his hazel eyes and looked at his old highboy dresser.

"Ah!" he groaned as he stretched both arms high over his head. *Another day. Yippee.*

"Good morning, Eric," Maggie said to the oval screen.

Treat Mete

And I'm here to remind you of the mess you left when you went away.

Maggie enjoyed the music blaring into Eric's headphones as it filled the box. She bobbed along while she worked. His thoughts were almost entirely consumed by the song as they mimicked the lyrics.

It's not fair to deny me of the cross I bear that you gave to me, you, you, you oughta know.

Eric approached the familiar large glass door that he passed through daily. Above the door in bold block letters was a pink sign that read 'Treat Mete.' He removed his badge from the back pocket of his Levi's and swiped it across the rectangular card reader beside the door. There was a faint beep and a click as the door unlocked. *Beep. Still employed.* He removed his headphones and pulled open the door. *I think this thing is getting heavier . . . or I'm getting weaker. I need to work out. Should I join a gym? I'd never go. Forget it.*

Maggie smiled and continued to catalog his thoughts. She had filed away plenty of castaways about fitness and many short-lived health-related ambitions. Just inside the door was a narrow room with a half-moon desk at the far end. Behind the desk was a short round woman with brown curly hair and glasses. She smiled when she saw him. *Oh boy, here we go. Walk fast.*

"Good morning, Mister Green Shirt," she said. *Seriously?*

"Good morning, Cathy," he replied. *Super creative as always.*

Every day the receptionist enthusiastically hailed Treat Mete employees with their own personal greeting that most often had something to do with how they looked or what they were wearing or carrying. Eric had been Mister Blue Shirt, Captain Cola, Señor

Grumpy Face, Bennie Bagel, Harley Hair Cut, Mister Black Shirt, Kid Khakis, Herbie Headphones, Mister Striped Shirt, Larry Long Sleeves, Señor Sack Lunch, Doctor Dockers, Sir Grins A Lot, Peter Plaid, and, his least favorite of all time, Major Muffin.

"How are you this fine morning?" she asked with habitual zeal. *Fine until two seconds ago.*

"Too early to tell," he replied. *Cathy Cat Sweater. You're better, than that Eric.*

Maggie grimaced. She did not like when Eric was snarky or rude, even in his own mind. Although he found it a great source of amusement, she felt it undermined what a kindhearted person he had always been. Of late his snark and sarcasm had permeated his communications, internally and externally. She worried this pattern was becoming the norm.

"Have a super sweet Treat Mete day," she said as he quickly rounded the corner.

What is her problem? Ah! Every day. Stop. Please. He followed the wide hallway down past the restrooms. A tall, balding man emerged through the men's room door and smiled at him. *Shiny.*

"How's it going?" the bald man said. *Does he wax that dome? Is that shirt pink or peach? I couldn't pull that off. Good for him.*

"Good," Eric replied. "You?" *I have to pee. I can wait. Maybe? Yeah, I can wait.*

"Living the dream," the man said as they passed by one another. *Hooray for cliché.*

With a frown, Maggie moved the words into the ever-full sarcasm file. The main hallway ended as it intersected with a much narrower hallway that ran perpendicular to it. Eric turned left and quickened his pace. *Just let me get to my desk. Why is everybody so chatty in the morning? Did I put on deodorant? There's the door. Almost there.*

Maggie continued to file and catalog as quickly as the thoughts displayed on her screen. She wanted to stay on top of it, since his thoughts often came in bunches and any backlog meant she would miss the action. She found even the most mundane task in his life delightful. She wished he knew how lucky he was and could behold the millions of souls who would gladly take his place even on his most dreary day. With his badge still in hand, he swiped it across the black pad on the wall to hear the sound of the familiar beep and click. He pushed the metal door open and stepped inside. *Uck. Is that fish?*

"Geez, Mark," he exclaimed. "What is that?" *Smells like a trash can on the beach. I'm gonna be sick. Why?!*

A stocky man with brown hair and a bushy mustache swiveled around in his chair to face the door. He wore a light blue button down shirt and held a small metal tin in his hands.

"Sardines," he said defensively. "Omega-3s, ya know? It's a superfood." *Gross.*

"It's 8:30!" Eric exclaimed. *Super food? Super smelly. Google omega-3 later.*

Maggie wondered what sardines smelled like. She wondered what it was like to smell anything. *I'm gonna quit this job. It's not worth it. Three years next to this guy. I'm gonna quit.* She could see his world in front of her and hear the varied and wonderful sounds but touch, taste, and smell were beyond her comprehension. *That stinking fish smell will be in his stache all day long. Kill me now.* She imagined that it must be a truly powerful thing to provoke such a reaction. *Take that nasty thing out of here.*

"And why are you eating at your desk?" he asked. *Again.*

"Did you watch *Better Call Saul* last night?" Mark asked, ignoring Eric. *No, say no.*

"Yeah, I watched it," he responded. *Here we go.*

"Here's my theory," Mark began. *Theory?*

"How can you have a theory?" Eric interrupted. "The show just started. And we know how it's gonna end. In a Cinnabon. In Nebraska! This isn't *Lost.*" *Enough with the theories. Calm down, Eric. That was an overreaction. You should apologize.*

"Geez, somebody woke up on the wrong side of the bed," Mark said. *It's GOT up on the wrong side of the bed, not woke up. And yes, I did.*

"I'm sorry, man," Eric said. "I didn't sleep well last night." *Or the night before.*

Maggie frowned, as she knew Eric was not being completely honest with Mark or himself. He slept fine when he eventually went to bed, but the past two nights he had stayed up late looking through a box of old photos and mementos.

"What's wrong?" Mark asked. "Tell Uncle Marky." *Uncle Marky? Is he serious? April. You know what's wrong. Think. You remember. It's somewhere in that sardine-addled brain. April. Ask me about April.*

Fifteen years Eric's senior, Mark fancied himself as a mentor of sorts. Despite a serious lack of validation and all evidence to the contrary, he considered himself endlessly witty and amusing. He had forged a counterfeit friendship with Eric in his own mind although Eric regarded him as a colleague who, at best, he tolerated in a semi-polite fashion.

"Just got a lot on my mind," he replied. *April. It's been a year. Ask me about April. Pink carnations. Brad. April. The park. I don't want to talk about it. Ask me about her. You remember. I know you do.*

The office door at the back of the room swung open and a lanky tanned man stepped out. His long sleeve shirt was neatly tucked into a pair of freshly pressed slacks that were barely held on to his bone thin frame by a dark brown belt. *Eat a sandwich or something.* The fluorescent light reflected slightly off his shiny brown penny loafers. *He must shine those daily.* His curly hair was gelled to perfection and his long face was clean-shaven. He put his hand on his hips and looked back and forth between Eric and Mark. *Fake bake.*

"Good morning, gentlemen," he greeted them. *Gentlemen is a bit of a stretch.*

"Morning, Bill," they replied in unison. *Say something about the smell. It's Mark. Get 'im Bill. How long does he spend on his hair?*

"Little Stalin lost another one," Bill announced. *Ugh. You've got to be kidding me.*

"Again?" Eric asked. "She just started last week." *Unbelievable. Dictator. Jerkwad.*

Maggie filed that in the pseudo curse folder and shook her head.

"Yeah, I know," Bill said. "He's got another temp starting this morning. Can you go set up her system ASAP?"

Isn't everything ASAP? "Yeah, no problem," Eric responded. *It'll get me away from the fisher king over here.*

"Thanks," Bill said. He turned to walk back into his office and stopped just inside. He turned back to the room with one hand on the door. "And Mark, take yourself and your nasty "superfood" down to the cafeteria. Nobody wants to smell that." *Boom. Justice served.*

Eric smiled as Bill closed the door to his office. Mark shamefully stood up from his desk and walked over to the door that led out into the hall. *That's right, fishy, hit the road.* He nodded to Eric with a sheepish grin and exited the room. *Finally.*

Eric placed his shoulder bag on the ground and pushed it aside with his foot. He sat down at his desk and pulled his keyboard closer to him. *Password. Heartless11. Time for Heartless12. Twelve months. I'm heartless. No pain.* He logged into his computer and waited for his desktop to appear. *You're not heartless. It still hurts. Boowhoo, Eric. Man up, Nancy boy.* He pushed his keyboard away in disgust. *Boot up you piece of junk. Need to defrag my box. Slow. Stupid. Come on.*

Maggie noticed his thoughts trended more negative in the morning. She had several theories as to why this might be, but without a mortal experience she had little evidence to back it up. In any case she did not enjoy Eric in this state. The majority of his morning thoughts were categorized as sarcastic, unkind, rude, intemperate, or inane. She was grateful that those categories tapered off dramatically as the day wore on. *I bet Bruce Wayne doesn't have to deal with a slow boot up. You know why? Cause he's Batman! How tall is Ben Affleck? Batffleck.*

The printer on the table behind Eric roared to life and a single sheet of paper rolled out onto the tray. Bill's office door opened and his well-groomed head popped out. "Little Stalin is calling. He wants to know when his new admin will be set up." *Tell him ASAP.*

Maggie quickly filed that under sarcastic.

"I just sat down, Bill," Eric said. *I've barely had time to lose all hope and slip into despair.*

"I know, man, but he's a VP," Bill responded. *VP of giant jerks.*

Eric found himself in an adult staring contest with his supervisor. *I'll go when I'm good and ready.* Bill simply smiled and waited patiently. He was an even-keeled man who Eric had never seen lose his cool. *Keep staring, I'm not moving.* With grudging admiration he considered Bill's cool, calm demeanor one of his boss's better traits. *Don't blink.* Eric gritted his teeth and pursed his lips but Bill continued to smile through closed lips. *Fine!*

"I'll get right on it," Eric finally relented. *I hate this job.*

"Thanks, man, you're the best," said Bill with a fake finger gun salute. *I hate you too. No, I don't. Sorry. Come on, Eric. What is wrong with you? Hair gel. Be nice.*

Eric got up from his desk and walked over to collect the paper from the printer. He looked down at the name. *Lindsey Jackman. She'll never last.* With the information sheet in hand, he made his way toward the door. *Sanctuary.* He reached up and touched the earphones that hung around his shoulders.

"Eric," Bill called from behind his office door. "No headphones, okay, buddy?"

Small talk. Headphones. White. Morons. Alanis Morissette. Why? Ugh. No. We're not buddies. Headphones. Spare me.

He pulled open the door without a word and stepped out into the hall. *Humanity.* Although there was no one to be seen, there were plenty of conversations emanating from the offices in both directions. *Quick and quiet.* He turned to his left and walked with purpose towards a large open area full of shoulder-high cubicle walls. *No eye contact.* He kept his head down as he hustled between the office cells. *You're a ghost. A ninja. A ninja ghost. Yeah. That would be freaking awesome.*

"Hey, buddy," called a voice from the last desk in the row. *Crud!*

"Quick question," said a rotund, red-faced man who was squeezed into his office chair.

"What's up, Carl?" Eric asked. *Besides your cholesterol. Yeah! Boom!*

With a tiny smirk, Maggie filed that under unkind.

"My computer won't let me log in," he said. *That's not a question. Wrong password.*

"Do you remember your password?" Eric asked. *Unlikely.*

"Yeah," he said. "It won't take it." *It would take it if you entered the right one.*

"Is your caps lock on?" *That's a shiny head too. Does he wax it?*

"No." *Then you don't remember your password.*

"Well I can't reset it from here," Eric explained. "You'll have to call support." *Is that a gravy stain? Headphones. Alanis, deliver me.*

"But you are support," he protested. *Yes, not a magician.*

"I'm not at my computer and I've got to go setup a new user right now." *Lindsey Jackman. Dead woman walking. Poor lady. Leave me alone. It's definitely gravy.*

He started to inch his way toward the corner of the cubicle. *Just call Mark. Or Bill. Use your phone.* He turned his head to look back down the aisle. He spotted Mark heading back from the cafeteria. *Don't do it. Too mean. You're better than that, Eric.*

"Hey, Mark," he called. *Nope, apparently you're not better than that.* "Can you help Carl with his password?" *And that stain on his shirt.*

Maggie stifled a giggle as she filed the thought and watched Eric duck around the corner without waiting for an answer. *Freedom.* He made his way down the hall to what was mockingly referred to as Executive Row. It was really just four consecutive offices occupied by the company's cofounders, the chief financial officer, and the vice president of marketing: Leonard Salmen, a.k.a. Little Stalin. Outside of each office, on the opposite side of the hall, were small cubicles where the admins sat. A support column came down right in the middle of the farthest cubicle, where the newest unfortunate would sit just outside Little Stalin's office. *Pathetic.* Eric shuffled by the square column and slid into the empty office chair. *This is a shoebox, not an office.* He placed the information sheet beside the keyboard and turned on the monitor. A glance over the half-wall countertop showed Little Stalin's door was shut. *Safe. Username: ljackman. Password: TreatMete10*

"You're not Sharon," a teasing voice called. *Here we go.*

He looked up from the screen at the middle-aged woman, who leaned around the column. *Perfume or bug spray?* She had purple-framed glasses and what looked like a fresh perm. *Janice.* "No, I'm not." *And you're not original.*

She snorted and waved a hand in the air. "I know that, silly man. Whatcha doing?"

Hating my life. You? "I'm setting up the computer for the new girl." *And hating my life.*

"New girl?" she asked. "What happened to Sharon?" *Take a guess.*

"Dunno," he said. *Fired. Quit. Ran off to Mexico.* "Just got a notification that the new girl starts today." *Didn't have time to warn her.*

"Well, Sharon didn't even last a whole week."

Yes, I know. We had a similar conversation when I set her up last week; it started with the same joke too. Eric shrugged his shoulders. *Please stop talking to me. Don't you have work to do?* He began typing on the keyboard and stared intently at the screen although it only displayed generic desktop wallpaper. *Somebody save me. Ring, phone, ring.* The phone in the next cubicle rang. *Wow.*

"Oh, that's me," she said and hustled off around the corner. *I'm magic. I have absolute power. Give me a million dollars.*

He opened his arms and looked up at the ceiling in anticipation. *Nothing. Dang.* With a frown, he put his arms down and went back to work. *Donuts. I should have summoned donuts. Much more realistic. Got greedy. My own fault.* He heard the sound of footsteps settle to a stop behind him and cringed. *She's back. I'm still not Sharon.*

"Excuse me," a timid voice spoke.

Eric spun around in his chair. He stared openmouthed at a slender blonde woman with long, wavy hair that fell across her shoulders. *April. Blonde. Looks just like her. Kinder eyes though. She's gorgeous.* She wore a gray, long-sleeved sweater over a teal shirt. *Pink. The park. Cheater. Heartless.*

"Hi," she said. *You're staring. Say something.*

"Hey'll," he stammered. *Hey'll? Hey'll?! What was that? It's "Hey" or "Hello." Get it together.*

She smiled and brushed a strand of hair off her cheek. He glanced down at the floor at the far corner of the cubicle. *No way out. Say something else. Ask her name. Say your name. Do something.*

"I'm new here and I'm not sure if this is where I'm supposed to be," she said.

Help her.

I hope not. He looked back up at her. *She's nervous. Help her. Smile.* He forced a smile and got up out of the chair. *Be smooth.*

"I'm Eric," he said as he extended his hand. *And you're beautiful.*

"Hail Eric," she said with a giggle as she raised one hand in the air. *Weird. Awkward.*

He could not contain the puzzled look on his face. Her cheeks turned red and she lowered her hand and folded her arms uncomfortably. "Like Hail Caesar," she muttered. "Stupid."

Cute. Hey'll. Hail. Save her. "You're not Lindsey, are you?" *Please say no, you adorable creature. Stop falling for her, Eric.*

"Yes, Lindsey Jackman," she sounded surprised. *She won't last a day. Stalin fodder. Pity.*

"I'm the IT guy," he explained. *Would you like to have lunch some time?* "I was just setting up your PC." *Too soon. April. Relax.*

Maggie watched in stunned silence. It had been quite a while since he had thought about a woman this way. She was all at once relieved and worried. Relieved that he might be moving on and worried there might be further heartache ahead.

"So is it all ready then?" she asked.

Already, what? Oh, all ready. "Yeah." *Good to go. Don't say good to go.*

He stepped to the side and she moved past him to sit down. *Flowers. She smells like flowers. What kind? Lavenders? Roses? She smells so good. Ask her what kind of flowers that is. No, don't do that.* She settled into the chair and rocked gently from side to side as she examined her tiny workspace. *She's so cute.*

"This is my first temp job," she said. "I'm excited. Is he nice?" *Who "he"?*

She gestured over the cubicle half-wall toward the closed door across the hall. *Little Stalin. The devil. Nope.*

"Who, Salmen?" he asked. *He's the worst. Run while you can.* "He's all right." *Liar. Tell her the truth. Warn her. He is the devil. El diablo.*

The door across the hall flew open. "Of all the brainless, stupid . . . ! I need a meeting with Wally. ASAP." *Great first impression, psycho.*

A mountain of a man burst into the hallway and glowered at the two of them. His dark hair was slicked back in meticulously straight strokes. A pair of beady eyes were sandwiched between his bushy eyebrows and matching mustache. *Monster.*

"Are you the new girl?" he bellowed. *You better watch yourself, fella.*

"Yes, sir," she answered meekly. "Lindsey Jackman."

She stood up from her chair and extended her arm over the counter of the half-wall between them. He looked her up and down, ignoring her greeting. *Animal.* "Great. Did you hear me? Set up a meeting with Wally. Like right now." *Are you kidding me? Give her a break.*

"Okay," she said, as she grabbed a pencil from the jar by her monitor and looked for something to write on. "A couple of questions. Right now, like set the meeting for right now or right now, like set it right now for later? Also, who is Wally?" *Uh oh, she doesn't know the president of the company. Not good. Tell her. Dead woman walking. Pity, she's pretty. April. Heartless.*

"Forget it," he scolded. "What a waste. I'll do it myself." *Lunatic. What is his problem?*

He stormed down the hallway and barked something at Janice before barging in to the corner office and slamming the door. *Despise. Punch him. Tell her it's going to be all right. Don't lie to her. Tell her the truth. Tell her to run.*

Help her.

The two words *Help her* displayed on Maggie's screen and drifted toward Eric. His thoughts always project out from him and were accompanied by his internal voice. Promptings, however, did not originate with him but came to him. To her they were dramatically set apart on her display but she wondered how Eric received them because much of the time they had little impact on his thoughts or actions.

"Sorry about that," said Eric. "He's a little . . ." *piece of garbage, insane, heretical, idiotic* ". . . intense."

"Yeah, seems so," she responded, still in shock. *Your job. Do your job and go.*

"Your username and password are on that paper there," he said, pointing to the printout on the desk. *Smooth. Say something nice, reassuring.*

Water formed in the corners of her eyes. *Please don't cry.* She sat back down in her chair and touched the paper with her slender trembling fingers. *Alabaster. Smooth. Delicate.* Then she turned back to him and flashed a bright smile. *Bright eyes, blue, light, gorgeous.* "Thank you so much," she said through tear-glistened eyes.

My pleasure. No. Twasn't nothing. Twasn't? What is wrong with you? Plus, double negative. It's 'twas nothing. Don't say 'twas. Good luck. Don't say that. "Good luck," he finally said. *Come on, Eric. At least you didn't say 'twas.*

He hung his head and slipped out of the cubicle before he could humiliate himself further. *Idiot.* With brisk steps and eyes purposefully forward he shuffled away from her like an over-anxious child shuffles out of the chapel doors on a bright on beautiful Sunday morning. *Don't run. Oh who cares, you've already humiliated yourself.*

"You too," she called after him over the half-wall countertop. *Me too? Me too, what?* If he had stopped or looked back he would have seen her pale cheeks turn red and flush as she settled back into the seat of her own embarrassment.

Maggie could not help but feel for the both of them as she continued to file Eric's thoughts with a particular delight in the awkwardness that had just ensued. She mused over his thoughts regarding her beauty and speculated what it might mean. It filled her with great hope that he might at last come to himself after sulking and mourning for over a year now. *What beautiful eyes.* The words flashed on the screen as Eric rounded the corner. Maggie filed them under admiration and attraction along with the thought that directly followed. *Such kind and beautiful eyes.*

Leapers

Eric drifted off to sleep much faster than he had the past few days. His last thoughts of the day were of the cluttered state of his apartment. He resolved in the abstract to do something about it soon, but no real target was set.

Maggie glided across the hall to the congreget. She immediately caught sight of her friends, Vila and Dae. They were conversing happily with Lorn. Lorn was an uncommonly bright spirit who worked in the regulet. Maggie suspected he had a particular affection for Dae as he always seemed keen to listen to her training stories, despite the fact that she seldom had anything of interest to report.

"Salutations, Maggie," Vila greeted her.

"Salutations, Vila," she responded.

"Salutations, Lorn, salutations, Dae," Maggie acknowledged the couple, so engrossed in one another they hardly noticed her approach.

"Salutations," they cheerfully replied in unison.

"Dae was just recounting the day her beholden had," Lorn explained.

"Yes," Dae began. "Many of her thoughts this day were on her children, particularly when they were younger; her little girl in pig tails and her son in short pants."

"And how is your beholden?" Lorn asked. "Does he still mourn Autumn?"

"April," Maggie corrected. "Actually something quite interesting happened while he was at work . . ."

"Pardon me," Lorn interrupted with a look out into the cosmos. "A turn is about to commence. Until our next."

"Until our next," Dae said as he passed through the light wall and out of sight.

Maggie and Vila stood silently by and watched their young companion gaze dreamily at the spot where he vanished.

Their congreget was much larger than when Maggie left it. Not being bound by actual physical limitations it could stretch and contract as necessary to accommodate the multitude regardless of its size. There were hundreds of spirits in the congreget now. Most of the curators swapped stories of their beholden while others simply listened enthusiastically. The practice was not encouraged but since it was not specifically forbidden either it was a practice engaged in with regularity. Some came to this place of gathering simply to study or play games, while others were drawn there to share in each other's presence. A busy-looking few from the regulet had business with a curator or processor and sought them out where they were sure to be found. There was an energy as they joined together that could be felt in no other setting.

"You said something interesting happened?" Vila said, breaking the silence.

"Yes," Maggie began. "A year has passed since April and . . ."

"Oh dear," Vila interrupted. "Excuse me, my sweet dove, Borador has just arrived and is of a sad countenance."

Vila wooshed to his side and engaged him with great urgency. Maggie was left to her disappointment with young Dae by her side, only partially present. Maggie observed the exchange between Vila and Borador for a moment before she settled down in front of the nearest oval platform and began to call up text from all that was known and recorded. She consumed the words like a cosmic vortex. Her favorite acts and deeds were of selflessness, heroism, and sacrifice. She had formulated a theory that where one was present the other two were sure to be found, in some measure or another. The records of the Only Begotten were well-founded and she had perused them many times but they did not compare to her own memories of singing in that heavenly choir as she bore witness herself to His birth. Her thoughts were interrupted as Dae spoke up from behind her.

"And how was your day, Maggie?" she asked.

Maggie looked up into her bright round face. In her question was all the sincerity and attention she had been denied previously. Still she chose not to hazard another unfortunate interruption.

"Fine," Maggie answered. "And yours?"

Dae looked nervously in Vila's direction and moved closer to Maggie.

"Of a truth there is little to report," she began. "Less than little. She just sits in a chair and drifts in and out of sleep. She thinks more of her cats than anything else, and they were parted some years ago. Maggie, it is dreadfully boring."

"She has lived a good long life," Maggie explained.

"And I saw next to none of it," Dae went on. "Vila talks of the rich and full life she led but that was prior to my arrival. Oh, Maggie, I wish I was assigned to you."

"Vila is a wonderful mentor and will show you all a curator needs to know."

"She is wonderful, and I love her, but her beholden . . . she . . . she is simply waiting for her turn to end."

"And when it does, Vila will go down and her turn will begin," Maggie said. "Dae, you will receive a beholden of your own in due course, and he or she will have their whole lives ahead of them. You will see and hear much, I promise. You must be patient."

"But what if I am assigned to a wayward?" she asked as they both turned to see Vila coaxing Borador in their direction.

"It is appalling," Borador declared. "An absolute tragedy."

"But they are his days," Vila replied. "He chooses what they will be."

"And I am to be subject to his waste until his days are utterly spent."

"He will give an account for that, but it is his turn."

Maggie and Dae looked over at their more seasoned colleagues. She had witnessed this back and forth between Vila and Borador many times before. This time, however, he seemed more passionate and upset. Vila was her usual calm and vibrant self and spoke plainly of the truth. While Maggie sided firmly with Vila, she could empathize with Borador, since she too had felt the emptiness of many misspent days and moments of Eric's time.

"He does not deserve his turn," Borador stated.

"That is not for you to say. Besides, he does not have to deserve it," Maggie interrupted. "And neither do you or I; it is a gift."

"If it is not earned, then why are we here?" he said and gestured around at the walls of the congreget. "Why must we wait? Why can I not take my turn when I please?"

"Everything is done in His time," Maggie replied. "There is an order and wisdom to His ways."

"This is truth, Borador," Vila added. "And you know it."

"But why does He allow those who would be so careless with His precious gift to go before those who would honor it?" he asked.

"He has given the gift freely, regardless of whether or not we would honor it," Vila said.

"I would not see it squandered on frivolous blather and mindless idleness. I would make better use of His gift," he argued. "Better use of my time."

"And so you shall," Vila said. "Be patient."

As the counsel echoed in her consciousness, Maggie looked over at Dae. Both she and Borador were similarly anxious, but their dispositions were dramatically different. Maggie thought of her beholden and how much easier it was for her to be patient because of him. Despite Eric's ordinary life, Maggie found herself fascinated with the details of the mortal experience. She was grateful that his mortal experience leaned more to the mundane rather than the profane. His thoughts at times bordered on the obscene, but he rarely dwelt there and did not care much for things of an immoral nature. Maggie knew her perspective would be quite different if Eric had made different choices with his life.

"My patience will not help him," Borador said. "I just want to make him understand, to make him do more. I want him to do better, to be better."

"Careful, Borador," Vila cautioned. "There is peril in your words."

"I am not a cast-out and I am no leaper," he argued. "I simply meant that he is squandering his probation, my desire is to help."

"What is a leaper?" Dae asked.

The three of them turned to their young friend and paused. Dae shrank slightly under the weight of their gaze. It was a question none took lightly. Borador and Maggie looked to Vila and waited.

"A curator and their beholden share a bond," Vila explained. "They are literally connected through the portal in the box. There have been some who would not wait their turn and exploited that connection. We call them leapers."

"I do not understand," Dae said.

"A leaper enters the beholden's mind through the portal," Vila explained. "They seek to take control of the body, to make it do their will. The body was never theirs to possess, though, and in the struggle the beholden is often driven insane."

"Why would He allow that?" Dae asked. "Is there not a way to prevent it?"

"That is not His way," Maggie spoke up. "As it has ever been, in all things, He allows us a choice."

"And what happens to a leaper?" asked Dae.

"At death the leaper is consigned to perdition," answered Vila. "With every choice there is a consequence."

The words hung in the air. It was nearly unimaginable to Maggie that someone would make such a choice. The thought forfeiting a body of her own was unimaginable and the idea of the end of her eternal progression was uniquely terrifying. None of them spoke or looked to each other. Maggie contemplated what might cause a soul to take such a drastic step. She considered Borador and all he had experienced in his tours at DOTAR. If there was anyone she knew who was capable of such folly, it was him. She began to formulate counsel that might quell him from entertaining any such thoughts, but at that moment Vila turned toward Dae.

"She is stirring," Vila said. "We must go. Until our next."

At these words she instantly disappeared through the nearest wall. Dae lingered for a moment with a worried look in Borador's direction before she turned to Maggie and said, "We are off to collect more thoughts of cats, until our next."

"Until then," Maggie said.

Dae followed after Vila, leaving Maggie and Borador amid a sea of curators. There was a low hum from the conversations all around them, but it was the void of communication between them that felt the loudest. Without so much as a glance in Maggie's direction, Borador settled over the nearest platform and began a game of quren. Maggie observed him for a time but thought better of proffering counsel that would not be well received in his current state. Instead she silently drifted out of the congreget and into the hall. Several spirits moved in and out of the passage traveling to and from their assignments. Maggie waited and watched until all was clear. She sailed to the end of the hall and through the wall at the far end.

Outside the department was a grand spectacle of stars and distant planets. She gazed up at a beautiful gold and purple nebula above her. The vast universe lay before her, which held unlimited possibilities and endless opportunities. But with no end to time and space, all these things could wait. What was most precious to her was the chance for a mortal experience and a physical body; if there was a pinnacle to the eternities, she believed that was it. She thought of Eric and all those who were, at this moment, on their own earthly journey. It was that journey that she treasured above all else now.

Far off in the distance a bright speck of light shone from a galaxy of eight planets, a sun, and a cluster of stars. Her thoughts immediately turned to leapers. She pitied those who could be so shortsighted to trade such a precious gift for a counterfeit and fleeting experience. She prayed for their souls and for those who were cheated out of their turn by the selfishness of a leaper. With one last look at her surroundings she returned to the white-walled facility of the DOTAR.

Lunch

Eric slumped down in his chair and stared at the collection of Treat Mete dispensers on his desk. *Knock off.* The mummy, Frankenstein's monster, and Dracula were the only truly recognizable characters in the lineup of oversized heads on sticks. On the far right there was one of a man with long brown hair that was supposedly Tarzan, but could have easily been a woman. Next to it was a plastic bust of a blonde girl that sat atop a light blue cylinder who he thought was Alice from *Alice in Wonderland* but might have been Jane or *Peter Pan's* Wendy. *It's Alice, definitely Alice.* A lion, a scarecrow, and a silver-faced metal man in succession alluded to the beloved characters from *The Wizard of Oz* but separately they could have been any lion, scarecrow, or silver-faced metal man because Treat Mete failed to reach a marketing agreement with MGM, Disney, or any media outlet who owned the rights to the iconic images the public might recognize.

The phone next to his monitor rang. *Not Mark, not Mark, not Mark.* He sat up and leaned forward to lift the receiver.

"This is Eric," he answered.

"Hey buddy, it's Mark," the voice on the other end said. *Crud.*

"What's up?" he asked. *He needs something, guaranteed.*

"I need a favor," Mark answered. *Yahtzee! What now?*

"I was just about to head to lunch," Eric said in an attempt to excuse himself. *Figure it out yourself. Eat a sardine. Ask your mustache.*

Maggie smiled at the thought of Mark talking to his mustache. She quickly shook off the grin and focused on her work.

"It will only take a minute," Mark said. *That's what you always say.* "Meet me down in shipping and receiving." *Say no. Think of an excuse. Something iron clad. Think, man, think.*

"Fine," he finally answered. *Eric, you are an empty-headed animal.*

"Thanks, pal, I owe you one," Mark said. *One? Try twelve.*

He hung up the phone and stood up out of his chair. *Tight.* While he stretched the muscles in his legs he surveyed the dispenser of the blonde-haired girl one last time. *April.* With a look over his shoulder, he retrieved his headphones from the desk and placed them in his ears. He removed his phone from his front pocket and plugged in the headphones underneath. *Colin Hay.* With a couple of flicks with his thumb he found the desired song and hit the play button. *Overkill.* The strum of acoustic guitar strings burst into life. Maggie began to bob along as Eric pulled open the door and stepped into the hallway. *I can't get to sleep, I think about the implications of diving in too deep, and possibly the complications, especially at night, I worry over situations, I know we'll be all right, perhaps it's just imagination.* He moved quickly and with purpose down the hall and through the threshold to a larger open area of cubicles and filing cabinets. *Day after day it reappears, night after night my heartbeat shows the fear, ghosts appear and fade away.* He pressed on his headphones and looked down as he passed two coworkers conversing in the hall. *Don't make eye contact. Walk faster.* Eric quickly rounded the corner and pushed through a large set of double doors. Several chain link cages were on his left. They were filled to the top with cardboard boxes with the pink Treat Mete logo printed on the side. Ahead of him was a forklift resting near the warehouse doors that led to the loading dock. *At least there's pretty lights, and though there's little variation, it nullifies the night from overkill.* Maggie heard a muffled voice above the music as Eric turned to his right. Mark stood by a white plastic folding table in the corner next to a box with a blue HP label and a picture of a printer. *Great. Back pain.*

"Over here, buddy," Mark waved to him. *We're not buddies.*

Eric slowly removed his headphones and made his way over to where Mark stood. He cautiously leaned over the open box and looked down. Inside was a heavy-duty laser jet printer walled in by styrofoam inserts. *Heavy.* He looked up at Mark who had a wry smile on his face and gestured down at the box with two opens hands. *Clown.*

"What do you say, boss?" Mark asked. "Can you help a brotha out?" *Don't do that, you're not hood. Let's get this over with.*

"Of course," he replied. *Glad to help. Truly. Just don't talk. Lift with the legs.*

"Thanks, bud," said Mark. *Ugh. Don't make me regret this. Lift with the legs.*

"Lift with your legs," Eric counseled. *Heavy. Back pain. Careful.*

He and Mark bent down together and reached inside the box. Their heads were close enough to touch. *Old Spice, a lot of Old Spice.* Eric grabbed hold of the bottom of the printer and tensed the muscles in his legs. *Lift with the legs.*

"Ready?" Mark asked. *No.*

Eric nodded in the affirmative.

"1-2-3," Mark counted.

On three they heaved upward. *Holy heavy printer, Batman.* They stepped toward the wall and plopped the printer on top of the folding table. *There goes the back.*

"Woo," Mark exclaimed. "Thanks Broseph, that was a beast."

You got that right. "Don't mention it," Eric replied. *No worries, you should have said "No worries." Don't mention it is fine though. It's fine.*

Offer assistance.

Two bold words appeared on the screen without the accompanying sound of Eric's voice. Although Maggie did not file promptings, she was intensely interested in what followed them.

"You need any help hooking it up?" *Please say no. And don't say Broseph.*

"Nah, I got this," Mark said. "You go to lunch." *I'm a jerk. Offer again.*

"Seriously, I don't mind," Eric offered. *Let me help you. Penance.*

"Nah, I'll have this hooked up in a jiffy," Mark said. *Who says jiffy?* "Go on to lunch. Save me a seat and we'll call it even." *A seat? I'd rather help with the printer. Stop being a jerk, Eric.*

"You got it," Eric said. *Now you have to sit with him. There are worse things. Be nice.*

Maggie filed and categorized quickly. She was thankful for the internal struggle and happy to see that his kindness had won out. In his lifetime, Maggie had cataloged far more positive thoughts than negative but his recent chart trended firmly toward the negative. She was grateful for the prompting and rejoiced in even a spark of his old self.

Eric stepped through the large twin doors and back into the office area. He put his headphones back in his ears and fished for his phone in his pocket. With the flick of his thumb he pressed the double arrows that pointed left and his song resumed from the beginning. There was an odd melancholy to the tune but the tone was a pleasant one. He passed another pair of coworkers on his way to the lunchroom and managed a polite nod of acknowledgement. *Hey.* They nodded back and he was grateful not to have to engage them in idle small talk. There were a half-dozen round tables scattered across the room with a vending machine and a soda dispenser next to a refrigerator along the same wall as the entrance. He made his way to the fridge and pulled open the lower door. The light illuminated a Slim Fast drink, two Gatorade bottles, one brown paper sack, and several lunch bags in a variety of colors. Eric reached in and retrieved the brown bag with his lunch in it. He turned around, closed the fridge, and surveyed the room for an open table. Janice sat at the table near the entrance with a dark-haired woman who was clearly upset about something. *What was her name? Peg? Penny? Pam? Dunno.*

"So I told him that wasn't happening," the dark-haired woman exclaimed. *Drama. Ignore them.*

There were four empty tables between them and the table in the corner where Eric usually sat for lunch. That table, however, was occupied by a tall, slender blonde woman reading a book. *April. No, Lindsey. Soft. Pretty. My table. Not today.* He looked back at the table where Janice sat. *Pam, I'm 90 percent positive, it's Pam. Avoid the drama.* He walked straight for the table next to Lindsey and sat down facing the wall. *Glad I trimmed my nose hair. Don't look. Peanut butter.* There was a bright yellow poster on the wall with an oversized Treat Mete dispenser of a man wearing a plaid deerstalker with a pipe in his mouth. The bold bubble letters spelled ELEMENTARY. *Knock-off Holmes.* He emptied the contents of his sack on the table: a boxed apple juice with a bendy straw, string cheese, and a peanut butter and jelly sandwich in a clear plastic bag. *Home. Mom. Safe.* With an intent stare, he straightened the juice box and carefully placed the string cheese parallel to his sandwich.

"It'll be a cold day in you-know-where before I do him any favors," Pam concluded her story as Janice's head bobbed along in accord. *Women are crazy. And scary.*

Eric carefully removed his PB&J from the plastic bag and rested it on top. Next, he tore the plastic from the string cheese and peeled a strand from the tube. *Don't look at her.* He chewed on the string cheese and looked blankly at the yellow poster in front of him. *Don't look.* As he glanced to his right, he caught Lindsey watching him from over top of her book. *Idiot, I said DON'T look.* She smiled and turned her attention back to her book. *Her smile. Her eyes. So pretty.* He nonchalantly picked up his sandwich and took a bite. *Chew casually. Be cool. You're cool. That's it. Nice chewing. Is she watching?* He looked back over to find her looking in his direction again. She gave a tiny nervous wave. *Cute.* Eric removed his headphones and smiled at her.

"Hail Eric," she said as she raised her arm slightly higher in a mini salute. *So cute.*

"Yeah, hey'll," he grinned. *Say something clever dummy.* "You got a book there." *Real clever. Moron. Just run away. Ah!*

"Yep," she said.

Maggie was greatly amused to see Eric in such a state. He prided himself on his quick wit and she was glad for the dose of humility being served to him.

"Do you read?" asked Lindsey. *Weird question.*

"No," he replied. *That sounds bad.* "I mean, I can read. I just don't. I mean I read, just not books." *Stop, you are making it worse.*

She grimaced and set her book on the table. *Save this. Tell her you read. Tell her you love it. Lie. No, be honest. Say something.*

"I have read books," he continued. *Good. More like that.* "I just prefer, uh, other mediums." *Nice save. That was it. Other mediums.*

"Like what?" she asked.

Movies. He took a bite of his sandwich. *Think of something more sophisticated.* He looked over his shoulder when he noticed the table behind him had gone suddenly silent. *Nosey.* Janice and Pam sat angled in his direction and peered at the two of them in a less than subtle way. *Eavesdroppers.* They briefly looked away and he turned back to his sandwich and took another bite. *Say the theater, that's sophisticated. You prefer the stage. Broadway. You've never been to Broadway. Quick, man, think. Speak.*

Don't say movies. "Movies," he replied. *Ah! She's going to think you're dumb. Change the subject.* "Do you like movies?" *That's the same subject!*

"Sure," she said. "I like movies." *I like your eyes. Focus, Eric.*

"Do you have any favorites?" he asked. *Say Star Wars and I'll propose.*

"I really enjoyed *Titanic*," she answered. *Ugh! Boo. No. Leo. Why?*

"That's cool," he said. *If you like horribly depressing endings. Change the subject.* "What's your book about?" *Now we're back on books. Way to go, genius.*

"It's kind of a mystery and part historical fiction about a treasure hidden in a forbidden island cave," she said.

That really does sound cool. Ask to borrow it. "Do you like it?"

"Very much," she answered.

"Cool." *Say something, besides cool. This is terrible. Ah, I've got nothing.*

She looked at him and smiled. *So pretty.* He looked back at her but still said nothing. A few moments passed and she awkwardly picked up her book and continued to read. *Gone.* Eric pulled the cellophane-covered straw from the side of his juice box and unwrapped the white bendy tube. He plunged it through the silver hole at the top of the box and held the straw to his lips. *Drink your shame.*

There was a screech and a shuffle behind him as Janice and Pam stood up from their table. The chairs scooted across the linoleum floor and Eric turned around. Neither of them looked over at him and they whispered to one another as the exited the lunchroom. *Bye.* All was silent again except for the slurping from Eric's juice box as he had drained the liquid from the bottom. He glanced back over at Lindsey who still had her head buried in her book. *It's over.* All he could see was her long wavy blonde locks. *I love her hair. You blew it, slick.* The low hum of the vending machines to his left was the only thing that broke the silence. He pulled apart the string cheese and chewed glumly. The specks of crumbs on the table offered a welcome distraction. *1, 2, 3, 4, 5, 6 . . .* He counted the crumbs to escape the awkward silence.

"Do you have a favorite movie?" she suddenly blurted out. *Is she talking to me?*

He looked up and quickly glanced around the room before his eyes fell on hers. *Answer her, slick.* "Star Wars." *And that's the end of that. She's probably going to laugh and run.*

"Oh," she said. *Oh, so you are a nerd. Yes, yes I am. It's been nice talking with you.* "I haven't seen it."

HAVEN'T SEEN IT?! You haven't seen it?! "You haven't seen Star Wars?" he shouted.

She looked startled and a little embarrassed. *Tone it down, psycho. Try again, like a normal person.* He opened his mouth to speak but before he could a voice sounded from behind him.

"Who hasn't seen Star Wars?" Mark asked. *Oh no. Go away. Not now.*

Mark dropped his lunch bag on the table, knocking over Eric's juice box. Despite there being five other empty chairs around the table, he chose the one directly next to Eric and plopped down. *Personal space. Geez, Mark.* Eric slid to the far side of his seat and leaned away from his new tablemate. *You better not have fish.*

"We were just talking about movies," Eric said. *Please don't mess this up.*

"Is this the new girl?" Mark asked as he opened the blue insulated bag and pulled out a rectangular tin. *Not sardines. No! Come on.* He cracked open the tin, rolled back the lid and pulled out a tiny, finger-sized fish. The smell immediately offended Eric's nostrils. *Gross.*

"My name is Lindsey."

He stood up from his chair and walked around the table. As he approached her he wiped his juicy fingers on the side of his pants and extended his hand. "I'm Mark." *And I stink of fish.*

Lindsey graciously shook his hand and smiled. *Oh, that smile. My heart. It's Beauty and the Beast.* Mark walked back to his chair with a big grin beneath his well-groomed mustache. "You're right, she's pretty," he whispered loudly. *Are you kidding me?! What are you doing? You lunatic. Kill me now.*

Eric shot a wide-eyed look at Lindsey, who blushed and looked away. Mark sat down next to Eric and continued, "So you've never seen Star Wars?" *Please leave.*

"Nope," she said. "Everybody is surprised when I say that." *Uh, yeah. It's Star Wars.*

"Eric here loves Star Wars," Mark offered with a pat on the back. *No touchy.* "He's even got Star Wars bedsheets." *You are killing me!*

Maggie could not help but feel sorry for Eric. Although she was far more intrigued by how Lindsey reacted in this exchange. She sat up straight with a pleasant look on her face. She leaned forward slightly and laid long looks on Eric while Mark was speaking. Maggie wished she could see Lindsey's thoughts as well. Did she like Eric? Eric seemed to be smitten with her, or at the very least he was interested. This was one of those times when Maggie felt truly powerless. She was strictly an observer with no real way to help or assist. The portal, she thought. At that, she glided past the oval platform and over near the portal on the wall. She moved in perilously close and felt an unsettling energy. She backed away slightly and stared at the scene before her. Eric sat with his arms folded and Mark sat beside him digging in the tin for another sardine.

"They are collectible," Maggie said aloud.

Collectible. "They are collectible," Eric said. *Brilliant, and technically true.*

"Nice," Lindsey said. "I have a collectible Fantasy Mickey figurine." *Not quite as embarrassing.*

Maggie moved back behind the platform. She was not sure if her words and Eric's thought were a coincidence or not. Could she communicate with him through the portal? Had she broken any rules? She was both excited and nervous. Vibrations rippled through her and she shook uncontrollably. She decided she would stay behind the platform from then on, per regulations.

"Cool," Eric replied. *Say something other than cool. You know other words.*

"Is that *The Land of Look Behind*?" Mark asked. *You just read the cover. You don't know this story.*

"Yes, have you read it?" Lindsey answered. *This just keeps getting better. If he's read this book I'm going to scream. Please say no.*

"No I haven't but I need to," Mark said. *Thank goodness for small miracles.* "I hear it has one heck of a twist at the end." *Dude, spoilers! Who does that? Come on.*

A look of disappointment spread across Lindsey's face. She looked down at the book in her hand and stuck her bottom lip out slightly. *Look what you did. She's still kind of cute when she sulks. Chide him.*

"Mark!" Eric finally spoke up. "Uncool. Let the lady read her book and quit spoiling it." *And quit smelling like fish. And learn to pick up on social cues. Or just stop talking in general.*

"I'm sorry," he said. *You should be.* "I don't know what the twist is. I just heard it's not what you expect." *Stop talking!*

"Come on!" Eric exclaimed. "Quit while you're behind." *Just quit.*

"Sorry," Mark said and he made a lip zipping gesture with his fingers across his mouth. *Finally. Now just keep those things zipped forever.*

"I'm really sorry," Eric said to Lindsey. *Let me make it up to you over dinner.*

"Don't worry about it," she replied. *Dinner. Ask her. Too soon.* "I love stories that don't end the way you expect them."

Eric looked up at the clock on the wall. *Time to make the donuts. Escape.* He carefully swept the crumbs from his sandwich into the clear plastic bag and returned it to his brown paper lunch sack. With habitual procession, the plastic bag was followed by his empty juice box and the string cheese wrapper. *Hurry before it gets any worse. Coward.* He stood up from his chair and pushed it gently underneath the table.

"I'd better get back to it," he said with a nod toward Lindsey. *Good-bye.*

"It was nice talking," she said. "Live long and prosper." *Huh?*

She held up her hand with her fingers separated into two pairs and explained, "Star Wars?" *Nope. Nice try though.*

"That's Star Trek," Eric responded and tried not to sound too judgmental. *It's okay, beautiful girl. Tell her it's okay.*

"Oh," she blushed. "Well, um, I really don't know Star Wars then."

"I know," he said in his best Harrison Ford impersonation. *Nailed it. She won't get that reference, dummy. That sounded bad. Tell her that was Han Solo. Tell her about Han Solo. Tell her about Bespin and carbonite. Ah! Nerd. She doesn't care. Just go.*

Without another word he turned and walked toward the exit. He crumpled his lunch sack, raised it over his head and tossed it toward the trash can in the corner. *For three!* It hit the side of the container and fell to the floor. *NO! Why did you do that? Pick it up. Don't look back.* He bent down, scooped up his failure and hurriedly placed it in the can. *Did she see? Don't look back.* He quickened his pace and continued to the doorway with his head hung down and his eyes fixed on the floor. *What a train wreck.* Someone brushed past him as he stepped out of the lunchroom and nearly knocked him over. *What the?!* He looked up and saw Leonard Salmen charging his way toward where Lindsey sat. *Jerk! Someone ought to teach him a lesson. Put him in his place. How 'bout you, tough guy?* As he continued his flight to his desk he heard the raised voice of Little Stalin. *Leave her alone. Come on, Eric, do something. Be a man.* With each step that carried him further away from the scene his shame grew. *Coward.*

Vila's Turn

She did not feel the usual draw to associate with her friends in the congreget. Instead she sought a place she had known before with a burgeoning scheme developing in her wake. The long hallway that led from her box ended in an expansive pavilion at the center of the department. Every hallway at DOTAR converged on the regulet. Spirits moved swiftly through the hub in all directions. Millions of tiny threads of light poured in from all sides and flowed up and over a central barrier. This circular barrier at the center of the pavilion sat atop the white floor like a ring made of light and encompassed the stewards, who directed the work among all departments. They ensured that all things were done in wisdom and order; every assignment went through them. Maggie approached the barrier and halted next to the nearest steward. A petite but bright spirit had just left his presence and he had turned his attention to the platform in front of him. Maggie drew nearer and awaited his attention.

"Excuse me," she finally spoke.

"Salutations, Maggie," he greeted her.

As a steward, he knew the name of each and every soul under the direction of the regulet; it was a gift granted them by virtue of their calling. Maggie had not met him before and felt at a disadvantage, especially considering what she had come for.

"Salutations," she replied. "And you are?"

"Forgive me," he said. "My name is Nalem. How may I be of assistance?"

"Pleased to meet you, Nalem," Maggie began. "I seek the curator assigned to a finite named Lindsey Jackman."

He regarded her without answering. She knew that her request was outside the realm of her call and would definitely be questioned and possibly be met with derision. Nevertheless she was determined to inquire and intended to be up front and honest about her intentions.

"May I ask why it is that you seek this particular finite's curator?" Nalem asked.

"My beholden has encountered Lindsey and I wish to commune with them about this shared encounter," Maggie stated plainly.

He studied her for a moment and his countenance hardened slightly.

"You are aware of the counsel against such an action?" he asked.

"I am," she replied.

"Then you know the potential hazards that lie in such a path," he continued. "Curators are not to become involved in the affairs of their beholden. You are a witness to their life, not a participant. To seek after more than this, you risk all."

"I understand," she answered.

"Very well," he said, after a long hard look. "Her curator is Kya."

"Thank you," she said with a slight bow. She turned to leave the regulet before she could receive any further admonitions. As she left she looked up at the starry heavens above and said a short prayer for forgiveness.

In an instant, guided by thought and desire, she was in the congreget. She discerned Kya's presence at once and drew close to a crowd of spirits by Kya's side. The group conversed softly and Maggie waited for a break where she might speak. She calmed her countenance and approached her objective.

"Kya?" she began. "May I speak with you?"

The tall spirit, with majestic flowing locks of light, turned to look upon Maggie. Her soft and welcoming expression dispelled all of Maggie's apprehension.

"Greetings, sister, tell me your name," she said.

"My name is Maggie," she answered.

"What can I do for you, Maggie?"

She had a queenly manner to her and an air of wisdom and grace. Maggie was dumbstruck because she had not expected to encounter a spirit of that magnitude. She briefly reconsidered her mission before finally screwing up the courage to speak.

"Eric Barkley is my beholden," Maggie explained.

"And you are here to speak of him?" she asked.

"I was hoping you would speak of Lindsey," Maggie said.

The glow from her person did not diminish or waver but Maggie sensed she was not pleased by her request. Still the expression on her face remained pleasant and so too remained Maggie's hope.

"There is little to be gained from such an exchange and much to lose," Kya finally answered.

"Please, if I could just know how she feels about him," Maggie went on. "Eric has been through a lot."

"So have all who have passed into mortality," Kya said. "To seek to satisfy every curiosity is to lose sight of our purpose. This is their time and we are but spectators. It is not for us to know all. Of a truth, it is right and good that we do not."

"I understand," Maggie said. While she had hoped to find a partner in curiosity she certainly did not expect to. All curators were counseled not to share the thoughts of their beholden and were warned of the potential dangers of doing so. Maggie felt her desires were pure but knew that Kya had spoken the truth.

"I am pleased to have met you, Maggie," she said. "Until our next."

"Until our next," Maggie said. Although she was disappointed, she could not help but admire this magnificent, faithful figure as she glided away. Maggie retreated to the far end of the congreget in search of solitude that would allow for reflection and contemplation. She found an uninhabited corner and settled in next to an oval platform. Her hope of learning how Lindsey felt about him now entirely rested with Eric. If he could muster the courage to pursue her then they would find out together if she returned his affection. So preoccupied with her obsession, she did not notice Dae's approach.

"Maggie, I am so pleased I found you," she said.

Maggie looked up into the bright face of her young friend. She glanced around briefly before asking, "Where is Vila?"

"That is why I have come," Dae explained. "Thelma's time is over. It is now Vila's turn."

Dae and Maggie both glowed with joy. This was a moment each curator anticipated and they rejoiced for their friend. Maggie thought of how she would miss Vila but could not have been happier that her time had finally come.

"Lorn has arranged for us to witness her commencement," Dae said, bursting with excitement.

"We have to find Borador," Maggie said. "It would grieve him to miss it."

"He is already with Lorn," Dae said. "They are waiting for us now."

With that they sailed out of the congreget and down the long hallway. They found Lorn and Borador near the center of the regulet. Borador appeared anxious and Maggie could not tell if he was pleased to see them or not. Lorn acknowledged them as they approached but quickly moved around the central barrier to the opposite end of the pavilion. The trio followed without a word and remained silent as they passed through the threshold to the sacred room beyond. A sense of reverence and awe fell upon Maggie as she beheld the place she had only heard of. There were a series of steps that bordered the confines of this space and cascaded down to the middle. A long shimmering veil stretched to the heavens in both directions and faded into the stars. Several spirits were gathered at the bottom of the steps near the veil while others gracefully gliding back and forth among them. They moved with great earnestness and purpose but in a calm and serene manner. Maggie spotted Vila on the edge of the group.

"Wait here," Lorn commanded in a whisper. He descended the steps and escorted Vila back up to them. Maggie had never seen her so full of joy.

"Salutations, my friends," she greeted them.

"Salutations, Vila," Maggie replied.

Neither Dae nor Borador spoke. They appeared to be awestruck by the moment. Vila regarded them warmly with a nod of understanding. Her time had come and her words were all she could leave with them for now. It was time to bid adieu to one another. She moved over to Dae first.

"Sweet child," she began. "You will make a fine curator. All that you have left to learn will be for your own benefit, to prepare you for your time. Your beholden will be in good hands, of that I have no doubt."

With a nod and a gentle smile, Vila glided over to Maggie.

"I have long admired your passion for learning," she said to Maggie. "As my time has come I wish now more than ever that I had a portion of what you have acquired. Although very soon my memories will be hidden from me, I believe you were right when you said our task down there is to remember. Perhaps we will remember one another should our paths cross."

"Until our next," Maggie said with a smile.

Vila nodded and moved over to Borador. Her expression turned solemn and the two regarded each other silently for a moment. Borador hung his head and looked away. Vila captured his attention with a slight lean toward him.

"You are a noble and great soul," she began. "Those things you have faced were given you because of your strength. Lesser souls would have crumbled under the weight but you did not. There is no shame in your time here and nothing is wasted. Your reward awaits you, Borador. Remember that and know of the truth."

Borador appeared taller and grander than he had ever seemed before. He glowed back at Vila with a brightness that rivaled her own.

"I love you," he said to her. "I will . . ."

Overcome with emotions he stopped short of speaking all that he felt. Vila moved in closer to him until their forms touched.

"And I you," she whispered.

Maggie looked away, not wanting to intrude on such an intimate moment. She noticed Dae had not done the same and gazed in their direction with glee and excitement. Maggie chastised her with a shake of the head and Dae dutifully looked away.

Two glorious figures glided gently up the steps next to Vila. They wore shimmering robes that matched the veil behind them.

"It is time," one of them spoke. Vila nodded and moved away from Borador.

"Until our next," she said to the group. "If you find yourself in N'Djamena, look me up."

The three of them turned and moved down the steps toward the veil. Borador started after them but Lorn moved in his way. As the two regarded each other, Borador's countenance dimmed again.

"Only those whose time has come can proceed beyond this point," Lorn explained.

"But what about them?" Dae asked as she gestured to the figures in shimmering robes who escorted Vila toward the veil. "Has their time come?"

"Their time has come and gone," Lorn said. "They are facilitants. They are souls so pure that they only remained briefly in mortality. As they now know the way, they are tasked with assisting all those who come after to begin their turn."

Maggie watched as Vila was led to the veil by the spirits in the shimmering robes. Vila was one of the most radiant spirits she had ever met and she wondered how long her turn might be.

"Is this true for all the pure?" Maggie asked.

"No," he said. "There are those whose time is as long as any other. Some are gifted, simple minds and kept innocent to protect them from the evils of the world. They are beacons of light in the darkness, a boon to all who know them."

There was a brilliant flash of light as each spirit passed through the veil. Vila conversed with her facilitants before she was at last ushered forward. With one last look back at her friends, she was enveloped into the veil and in a glorious burst of white she passed into the next estate. Maggie was overjoyed for her friend but at the same time felt profound sadness from her departure.

"We must go," Lorn said.

Dae and Lorn turned and departed from the room the way they had come. Maggie began to leave but stopped when she noticed Borador had not moved. He stood right where Vila had left him and stared toward the veil. Maggie moved close to him.

"We will see her again," she said. "Perhaps during our own turn."

He shot her a forced smile of gratitude and turned and left without a word. Maggie observed the flashes of light as one spirit after another began their turn. She dreamt of the day when she would return to this place to begin her own turn. With that happy thought she turned and followed Borador back across the threshold to the regulet.

Dave

S*have.* He looked in the mirror at the brown stubble that covered his face. *Did I shave last week? Yeah. Wait no. I can't remember. It's time. Shave, you slob. It's Saturday. Shave tomorrow. He rubbed his whiskers. Or you could grow it out, might look cool. It will look patchy. Just shave.* There was a small white scar on his chin that he'd had since childhood. *Skateboard.* He rubbed it gently with his thumb. Maggie remembered the day he suffered the injury when he lost his balance trying to catch hold of a passing pickup truck. *Nothing's ever going to grow there.* He smiled broadly and examined his teeth. *Beautiful.* He turned on the faucet and picked up the soap next to the sink.

Maggie wondered what soap felt like. The solid lime green block turned shiny. White foam formed all around it as he rubbed it between his hands beneath the water. As he turned off the water there was a distinct clicking sound from the front room. *What's that?* It was followed immediately by a crash as something fell to the floor. *What was that? Someone's in the house!*

Eric looked anxiously out from the bathroom. *Stay calm. Bat. Bedroom, get to your bedroom.* He moved to the door with his back pressed firmly against the wall. *Breathe.* With a deep breath he leapt into the hall and bounded through his bedroom door. His toe struck the side of the door jam and he fell against the foot of his bed. *Filth, that hurt. Filth and foul, filth.* He pursed his lips and did not make a sound. *AH!* With a slight limp he hobbled over to his closet and gently slid the mirrored door to one side. *Bat.* He reached inside and retrieved a black wooden bat from the corner. *Joey. Slugger. Go time.* More sounds of movement came from the front room. *Intruder.*

While she continued to do her job and moved his thoughts into the proper files she could not help but worry for him. She could not fully appreciate what it was to be in mortal danger, but the idea of a turn being cut short was something she completely comprehended. She worked frantically and seemed to be drawn ever closer to the portal in front of her.

With his back again pressed against the wall, he stepped sideways into the hall. *Quietly. Softly. Ninja.* He crept forward slowly with the bat raised just above his waist. A clanking of glass bottles sounded through the one-bedroom apartment. *Kitchen. Fridge. He's in the kitchen. Or she, don't be sexist. A girl wouldn't break into your house. Keep dreaming.* He crossed to the opposite side of the hall by the bathroom door. *Breathe.* He raised the bat over his head and bent his knees slightly. *Strike hard, strike fast, no mercy.* In one quick motion he sprang around the corner unto the linoleum floor of the kitchen. *Be scary.*

"Freeze, dirt bag!" he shouted. *Dirt bag?*

The large man who leaned into the open refrigerator jumped up and bumped his head on the freezer door. He moaned and grabbed the back of his head as he fell backwards on his rear end knocking the refrigerator door against the wall. The glass bottles in the door clanked again as they knocked into one another. *Dave?* The man wore an orange tie-dyed shirt and blue jeans. He had a long shaggy beard and a round face. *Flipp'n Dave!*

"Dave?" Eric asked. "You scared me to death!" *Lunatic.*

"Me?" Dave said, with his hand still rubbing the back of his head. "I nearly pooped my pants. What's with jumping out on a brother like that?" *Are you kidding me?*

"Are you kidding me?" Eric replied. "What are you doing?"

"It's Mario Kart day," he answered. *Oh yeah. Wait, not relevant.*

Eric lowered the bat and walked over to his friend. He reached down and helped him to his feet. The light from inside the fridge illuminated the dark brown cabinets of the tiny kitchen.

"What are you doing in my kitchen?" he asked. *It's early.*

"Well I picked some bell peppers from my garden and I figured you had eggs so I thought I'd make us some omelets," he replied innocently. *Mmm, omelets. Focus, Eric. Stay on point.*

Dave pointed to three green peppers on the kitchen counter next to a chrome toaster.

"But how did you get in?" *Did I forget to lock the door?*

"Oh, I just crawled through your window," Dave replied. *Of course you did.* "Your screen pops right off and the window slides open. You should really consider locking that." *Oh I will. There's a joke here somewhere. Breaking eggs, breaking and entering. I got nothing. Moment's passed. Moving on.*

The morning light seeped in through the front window. The lampshade on the end table was slightly askew and the collectible Imperial AT-AT lay on its side. *That better not be broken.*

"Why didn't you just knock?" *You know, like a normal person.*

"It's early and I didn't want to wake you if you were still sleeping," he said. *Why is it that every person I know is insane? Maybe it's me.*

"That's very thoughtful," he said. *You crazy person.* "But I nearly killed you."

"You? With a baseball bat?" he laughed. "I'll take my chances." *What's that supposed to mean? I could take you, ya big lug.*

Dave was a tall man with a broad chest and shoulders. He had shaggy, unkempt hair and a crooked smile. Although he was physically imposing with an undeniable strength, there was a gentleness to his demeanor. He reached back into the still open fridge and pulled out a carton of eggs. *Help yourself, Dave. Omelets.* Eric set the bat on top of the counter and reached in the cupboard next to the sink. He pulled out a cast iron skillet and placed it on the nearest burner atop the stove. *Breaking and omeleting. There it is. Dang it, I missed my window. Pity.*

"How about a southwestern omelet?" Dave asked. *Yeah. Tasty.*

"Sounds good." *Might as well roll with it.*

"You got any ham?" asked the big burly intruder. *Ham too?*

"What exactly are you bringing to this party?" Eric demanded. *Besides body odor.*

"These are fresh picked peppers from my garden," Dave stated proudly. *Right, your "garden."*

"Is this the same garden you grow your 'herbs'?" Eric said with sarcastic air quotes.

"That's medicinal, man," he argued. "You know that. Besides I keep that separate from my veggies. Do you have ham or not?"

"It's in the meat drawer," Eric said and pointed to the still open fridge. *Close the door. You are letting all the cold out. You sound like Grandpa Steve. You're letting all the bought air out.*

Dave pulled open the drawer and removed a plastic bag full of pink juicy ham. Underneath it was a bag of yellow shredded cheese. Without asking, Dave took the cheese as well and at last closed the refrigerator door. *Cheese too, why not.* Eric turned on the burner beneath the black skillet and grabbed a small plastic bowl from the cupboard overhead. Dave cracked the first egg and carefully poured the contents into the bowl. While Dave was cracking the second egg, Eric pulled a fork out of the drawer to his left.

Everything about food fascinated Maggie. She was completed captivated by the look of it and all the energy that finites put into obtaining and preparing it. In her estimation there was little on Earth that could match food for its importance and universal appeal.

"How about onions?" Dave asked. *Onions too? Come on, man.*

"Don't you have onions in your garden?" he questioned. *Free loader.*

"They aren't ready yet," he responded. *Of course not.*

"Well I don't have any onions." *Or patience.*

"Well I guess these won't be very southwesty then," Dave mumbled under his breath. *Is he joking? Throw him out. No, eat his omelets then throw him out. Mario Kart. Okay, right after Mario Kart I'm throwing him out.*

Dave handed Eric the bowl of eggs and pulled a knife from the drawer. Eric began to beat the egg yolks vigorously while Dave deftly cubed the peppers and ham and tossed them into the skillet. *Whoa, he's got skills. Gordon Ramsay over here. Smell's Kitchen. Iron Pest.* When Eric finished with the eggs he poured them on top of the peppers and ham and watched them sizzle. *Your brain on drugs.* Dave hopped up on the counter opposite the stove with childlike agility.

"So what's new, chickadoo?" he asked with a wry smile. *Chickadoo? He's one of a kind, that's for certain.*

"Nothing," Eric replied. He pulled a spatula from the drawer and dutifully manned the skillet. *Lindsey, tell him about Lindsey.*

"Noth'n?" Dave questioned. "I haven't seen you for a week and you've got noth'n? Brother, you're doing it wrong." *Tell him.*

"Some of us have jobs, we can't all spend our days in search of something new," Eric chastised. *Hobo.*

Maggie frowned. Not at what he thought but at the words he said. She imagined that her time would be filled with new and wondrous things. The idea of a life of monotony for her or Eric, or anyone, was harrowing.

"That's exactly what I mean, man," Dave continued. "You're wasting your life away in a box and for what?" *Money. Shelter. Clothes. Eggs.*

With the spatula, Eric peeled the edges of the omelet away from the sides of the skillet and started to turn it over.

"Hold up, man," Dave said as he leapt from the counter. "I like the cheese on the inside."

He reached over Eric's shoulder and grabbed the plastic bag. Still leaning against Eric, he extracted a handful of cheese and sprinkled it over the eggs and pepper. *Personal space.*

"You wanna do this?" Eric asked more than slightly annoyed. *Mr. Omelet.*

"Nah man, you're doing great," he said as he retreated to the other side of the kitchen.

That's right I AM doing great. Eric folded the omelet in half and covered the pile of cheese inside. He scraped along the bottom and dislodged the other side from the skillet. *This is how it's done.* Dave returned to his perch on the counter and watched Eric with great interest.

"Maybe I have something new but I just don't want to share," Eric said with faux derision. *Ask me. Ask me and I'll tell you.*

"Oooh, Mr. Secret," Dave taunted. "So out with it then, what's your thing?" *Well now I'm not telling you, Mr. Funny Guy.*

"No, you don't deserve it," he replied. *There, take that. That'll teach you.*

"You got noth'n," Dave shot back. *I've got a job and an apartment, you've got nothing. Except green peppers.*

Eric took a plate from the cupboard and scooped the fresh omelet onto it. He reached back without looking and handed it to his quasi-uninvited guest. Dave produced a fork from his pocket and gleefully accepted the plate. He cut off the corner of the omelet and took a bite. Meanwhile Eric had already tossed the next batch of cubed peppers and ham in the skillet and began cracking a pair of eggs from the carton. *Careful. No shells.*

"Good stuff, brother," Dave said as he swallowed his first bite and shoveled the next in his mouth. *Slow down, turbo.*

He whipped up the eggs and poured them on top of the peppers and ham. Dave continued to scarf down the egg, pepper, ham, and cheese infused semicircle. Eric began to fold over his omelet when Dave shouted, "Cheese!"

"I like my cheese on top," he replied. *This is my omelet.*

"Suit yourself," said Dave. *I will suit myself.*

Dave returned his attention to his plate and Eric continued his process. After he had flipped the omelet, he applied a generous helping of shredded cheese to the top and plated it before it melted. He walked around the counter and took a seat on the stool looking back into the kitchen. Dave finished his omelet and laid the plate in the sink. *That was fast.*

"I saw some OJ in the fridge," Dave said hopefully. "May I?" *Sure. Of course. Why not?*

"Yeah, big guy, go for it." *Can I get you anything else?*

Dave hopped off the counter and poured himself a glass of orange juice from a red container with a white duck on the side. He returned the container to the refrigerator and gulped down the orange liquid. *Why sure, Dave, I'd love some OJ. Thanks for asking.*

Maggie filed that under sarcasm. When she was in training she did not immediately recognize the sarcastic thoughts from the sincere, but by being Eric's curator for nearly twenty years she was now an expert.

"You ready to kart it up?" Dave asked as he placed his cup in the sink next to the empty plate. *Can I finish my flipping omelet first? Geez. Ha ha, flipping omelet.*

"Fire it up, I'll be there in just a minute," Eric replied. *Ah man, he's going to be controller number one. Relax Eric, it's fine. Did you change the batteries? Oh well. Too late now.*

Dave left the kitchen and walked over to the small front room. A flat screen television sat on top of a short shelving unit. He turned on the TV and pressed the power button on the white Wii unit on the shelf. Eric quickly finished his breakfast and dumped his plate in the sink. He hurried over to the futon and retrieved the controller from the floor. *Controller numero uno, baby. Take that.* Dave picked up the remaining controller and sat down next to Eric on the shabby blue futon. *Let's do this.*

"You ready?" Eric asked. *Koopa Troopa, Standard Bike L.*

"Ready to kick your butt," Dave responded. *Okay, tough guy.*

Maggie bobbed up and down to the music as Eric and Dave beeped and bopped through the screens of colorful characters and vehicles. *Moo Moo Meadows.* Eric selected a green and brown course with black and white cows in the road. *3 . . . 2 hold 2 . . . 1 GO!* They both held their controllers at chest height and began to maneuver the character on the screen in front of them.

"How's work?" Dave asked. *Do you really care?*

"Good." *Could be worse. Think of something to ask him. Vegetables?*

A smile broke across Dave's hairy face as Eric leaned into him and they both leaned forward intently. *Mushroom. Mushroom. Need a mushroom.*

"Do anything fun this week?" Dave continued. *Not really. Yes, golden mushroom! Hit it! YEAH!*

2,2,2,2,2,2,2,2,2. Eric repeatedly tapped a button on his controller in rapid succession. *Winning. 1st place.*

"Not really," Eric answered. "You?" *Cow.*

He leaned hard to the right, lifted his foot off the ground and held it high in the air. *That was close. Stinking cows.*

"The other day I jogged from Sutter's Fort to Sutter's Landing," Dave said. "That was fun." *You jog?*

"That's like not even a mile," Eric replied. *Lap 2. Red shell, come on red shell.* "Why were you jogging?" *Here it comes. Cops.*

"So I was minding my own business when this cop car pulls up next to me," Dave began. *Called it.* "He didn't say anything or even roll down his window, he just sat there." *Bananas.*

"Maybe he was just parking," Eric said. *Bananas.* He tapped his controller three times.

"Shoot!" Dave exclaimed. "Doggone banana!" *Heehee.*

Eric smiled as Dave jumped out of his seat and nearly fell to the floor when he tried to sit back down and missed the corner of the futon.

"Nah, man," Dave went on. "He was after me. I know it. So I faked like I was stretching and then started jogging." *Why?*

"What was your plan?" asked Eric. *Crazy. Dumb question. Gopher. Avoid the gopher.*

"I figured he wouldn't follow me if he knew I was onto him," Dave said. "Sure enough, he just sat there as I jogged away." *Because he wasn't following you! One lap to go.*

"Then why did you jog all the way to Sutter's Landing?" *Exercise? Green shell. Useless.*

"I needed a place to ditch him," Dave explained. "I jogged until a saw a bench next to a trash can. I Superman dove over the bench and rolled behind the can. I was lightning-quick, no way he could have seen it coming." *Because he wasn't following you. Let it go, Eric.*

"I've been thinking about jogging," Eric said almost as an afterthought. *I really should.*

Dave paused the game and turned to face Eric. *Hey, I was about to win!* "What's her name?" he questioned.

"What?" Eric asked. *Unpause the game. Lindsey.*

"There's only two reasons to workout," Dave said as he pointed his finger at Eric. "Fear of death or to look better au naturel. Are you dying?"

"No." *Not that I know of.*

"Then what's her name?" Dave demanded. *Lindsey.*

"I just want to lose some weight," Eric said in an attempt to deflect his friend's interrogation. *Just tell him. He's not going to stop.*

"Bull," Dave argued. "You're fine. This is about a girl." *Just tell him.*

Eric squirmed in his seat and looked over at the lamp by the window. *Lie.*

"There's no girl," he lied. *Why did you do that? Just tell the truth.*

"Look brother, April broke your heart," Dave said. "That's the worst, but it's been a year. If you're into some new hot chica, that's a good thing." *Hot chica? Who are you? Tell him.*

"Fine, there's a girl," Eric admitted. *Here it comes.*

"I knew it!" Dave shouted and stood up in the futon with a fist pump to the ceiling. He pointed and smiled at Eric. "Ha!"

Calm down. "Calm down," Eric ordered. *And sit down.* "Nothing has happened yet. There's just a new girl at work and I kinda like her." *A lot.*

"Name?" Dave asked again. *Oh right.*

"Her name is Lindsey." *Lindsey Jackman.*

"She sounds hot," Dave added. *You can't possibly tell by her name. She's beautiful. Change the subject. Back to the game.*

"Can we please finish the race now?" asked Eric. *I want to beat you.*

"No way, man," Dave said and held his controller over his head, out of Eric's reach. "Details." *None of your business.*

"There's nothing to tell," Eric said. "We've only talked a couple of times. She's pretty. She seems nice. She's kind of shy, I think. Oh and she's never seen Star Wars." *Her eyes. You didn't mention her eyes. Or her wavy hair. Blonde. Tell him she really is hot. Don't say that, Eric. You are better than that.*

"Wait," Dave said. "She's never seen Star Wars?" *I know, right? Tragic.*

"I couldn't believe it either," Eric said. *I mean, who hasn't seen Star Wars? Luke. Han Solo. The Millennium Falcon. Yoda. Chewbacca. Princess Leia. Lightsaber.*

"There's your in, man," Dave said. "Take her to see Star Wars." *Where?*

"It's not like it's playing in theaters," Eric replied. *You own it.*

"It's playing right here at Casa de Barkley," Dave answered. "Don't you have the silver deluxe Blu-ray edition or some junk? Invite her over for some screen time and popcorn and may the force be with you, ya know what I'm saying?" *Nobody knows what you're saying. It's not a bad idea. Courage. You could try it.*

"That's not a bad idea," Eric said. "I might have to give that a try." *Be smooth, like Harrison Ford smooth. "Hey babe, do you want to come back to my place and watch Star Wars?" Don't say babe. You're not smooth. Be yourself.*

"Do or do not," Dave said in a high raspy voice. "There is no try." *Walked right in to that one.*

"Fine," Eric relented. "I'll do it. Can we finish the race now?" *You're gonna lose.*

Satisfied, Dave sat back down on the futon and rested his forearms on his knees with the controller pointed at the television. "You ready?" *I was born ready.* Eric nodded and Dave resumed the game. There was an immediate alarm like beeping sound. *Blue shell. NO! I'm so close.* A blue streak hit the tiny green motorcyclist and launched him into air. *No! Come on!* A fat man in a yellow hat and yellow overalls sailed past him on a motorcycle while Dave giggled.

"And that's how it's done, chump," he exclaimed. *Lost. Loser. Grrr.*

Eric threw his controller to the ground. *Stink'n blue shell. Ah!* Dave stood up and stretched his arms gleefully above his head with a big yawn.

"You got anything to drink besides OJ?" he asked. *Water. Freeloader.*

"Water," Eric answered. *Why don't you drink your bell peppers? Eric, that doesn't make sense.*

"Let's walk down to Quik Mart and get a couple of 44-ouncers," Dave suggested. "And maybe some It's-Its, you know some racing fuel." *Let me guess, I'm buying. I am thirsty. It's-It. Yes. Always yes.*

"Sure," he said. "Sounds good." *Keys.*

He stood up and grabbed his keys off the kitchen counter. Dave walked to the front door and pulled it open. Eric looked to the front window as he crossed the room. He stopped in the doorway and looked over at his burly friend. *Leave him a key. Maybe a bad idea.*

"I'm gonna leave a key under the mat for you," Eric offered. "Don't climb through my window again." *You crazy hobo.*

"All right, sounds good," Dave said with a grin. He put his arm around Eric and escorted him out the door. *I'm going to regret this I know.*

Ties that Bind

Maggie left the box feeling empty from the day Eric had wasted on his futon. He and Dave played games until it was very late. They ordered pizza and had it delivered to minimize any disruption to their recreation. Much of his thoughts had been dedicated to frivolous and inane details about power boosts, squid ink, and his race-to-race ranking. Maggie yearned for him to make different choices with his time. She wished he realized what a gift it was that he was wasting. Her mood lightened however, when her thoughts turned to their conversation of Lindsey and the thoughts it brought to Eric's mind.

She crossed the hall and entered the congreget, which had swelled to lengths beyond her field of sight. It was at this moment she remembered that she would no longer find Vila there. Her feelings quickly turned from sadness to joy as she thought of her friend in her mortal tabernacle and all the wonders that she was sure accompanied it. She looked around until she spotted Borador, hovering over a platform, in the middle of the congreget amongst the throngs of spirits. Without hesitation she made her way toward him.

His countenance had dimmed slightly since the last time she saw him. On the platform in front of him a bright white orb bounced back and forth within the oval sphere. It did not have nearly the velocity that she had witnessed previously. It was as if the game had adopted the melancholy nature of its perpetuator. Maggie paused for a moment and thought of what she might say. She glided around to the opposite side of the platform from where Borador stood and smiled.

"Salutations, Borador," she said brightly.

"Salutations, Maggie," he responded politely.

"How is your game going?" she asked.

"All is well," he replied, although there was no feeling in his voice.

Maggie searched for words that would gladden and uplift him but none came. She had not known how deeply he cared for Vila until they said their good-byes. Vila had always been kind to everyone and her love was extended to all. Borador, however, was a different being altogether and had shown no real affection for anyone, that is until Vila was about to leave him. When it became apparent that she would find no tidings of joy she instead spoke for herself.

"I miss her too," she said.

He looked up at her and the energy platform quickly faded to a dull state. They shared in the moment together without saying a word. Maggie ached for him but knew there was little she could do to unburden him from his grief. His gaze was down at the white floor beneath their feet. When it became clear that there was nothing more to say on the subject Maggie determined to shift his focus.

"How is your beholden?" she asked.

"He is very much the same," Borador responded glumly.

"Eric spent most of the day staring at a screen and racing against a mustached villain with a tiny turtle riding a motorcycle," Maggie reported. "I know that upsets you. We could talk about that."

"Vila was right," he replied. "It is a perilous thing to dwell on such thoughts. They have their turn and it is given unto them to act as they will."

Disappointed in her vain attempt to change his emotional state she sought a different approach. She moved around the platform and stood near Borador until he looked at her. When she had his full attention she smiled again. He could not help but smile back although he tried to resist.

"There," she said. "That is better. Do you want to talk about her? We could share the things we miss most."

The smile faded from his face and he looked down once more. When he did not readily answer she continued.

"I'll go first. She was the first to greet me when I arrived at DOTAR. There was a large group of us and we were all lost. She came up to me and was so kind and loving. She showed me around and told me, 'Ours is an important work; we are entrusted with the thoughts of those who have gone before us. These thoughts will shape who they are and what they will become. Do not let yourself forget that or become discouraged by the trivial or the mundane. In the end, nothing is lost to Him.'"

She could not tell if her words had helped or hurt him. He still did not look up and his countenance had not changed from her arrival. She allowed time for him to speak but was met with only silence. She tried again.

"It was she who introduced me to you that day," Maggie went on. "For that I am eternally grateful; for you, Borador, are my friend. And we are still here for one another. I am here for you."

He still did not speak. Maggie had run out of ideas and her hope had all but evaporated. She waited awhile longer and tried to send as much positive energy as she could his way. He just stared blankly at the white sheet of light beneath their feet. She was about to turn and leave when he moved slightly.

"I miss her warmth," he said finally.

Maggie remained still and wisely silent. She waited and listened. At last he looked at her.

"I did not even know I was cold until I met her," he continued. "Things were what they were. She brought with her something that changed that. I craved her company, I needed it. Without it I . . ."

His voice trailed off. A far off look fell upon his face. Maggie knew what he was speaking of. Vila was radiant and her presence could literally be felt, even to beings of spirit. It was then that Maggie realized his pain was more than just the separation from a friend or someone he loved deeply, he felt a void in his being that only she could fill. There was nothing either of them could do except press forward in anticipation of an eventual joyous reunion, but she imagined that telling him those things would do little good.

"Everything has changed; things will never be the same," he concluded.

"No they will not," Maggie said. "They are not meant to be. We move forward and things change. This is the way it was intended to be."

"I know," Borador replied. "I do not begrudge her of her turn, truly I do not. But her presence made this state easier to bear and without her I . . . I am alone."

"You are not alone, Borador," Maggie said. "I am here. Dae is here."

"Thank you," he said as he brightened slightly. "I am grateful for that, but you and Dae are just reminders of what we now lack."

Borador turned away from her and swiftly sailed toward the nearest opening. He passed by Dae who had just entered the congreget. She greeted him warmly but he barely stopped to acknowledge her. Once he had disappeared, Dae looked to all sides until she spotted Maggie. She flew to her with great haste.

"Maggie!" she shouted. "Great news!"

With her thoughts still on the recently departed Borador, she struggled to switch gears and match her young friend's enthusiasm. She smiled and politely turned her attention toward her with a portion of her intellect continuing to process her last interaction.

"What news, my sweet dove," she heard herself speak the name Vila had given to her.

"I am to be Vila's curator!" Dae exclaimed with glee.

"That is wonderful news," Maggie exclaimed. She lit up at the announcement.

It was not common for a mentee to be assigned to her mentor but Maggie had heard of it happening before. This news brought joy for a variety of reason. She was pleased that Dae would no longer have to wait and wonder about her assignment, and she was relieved that she would not have a wayward. She could not imagine Vila making such heinous use of her gift. Finally, she was happy she would get to learn details of her friend's turn firsthand from her curator. Immediately she thought of Borador.

"Have you told Borador?" she asked.

"I tried to but he seemed to be in a hurry to leave," Dae replied with a slightly troubled expression.

Maggie looked back toward the last place she had seen Borador. She wanted to hasten to his side and share this beautiful news that would be sure to please him. Why had she not considered this as a possibility? There was the hope she searched for and it had already been realized. If she had only thought of it sooner or if Dae had arrived moments earlier, for now she would need to be patient. She already began to construct how they would break this joyous news to him when Dae continued.

"There is more good news," Dae said.

"More?"

"Yes," she beamed so brightly that Maggie wondered if she would burst. "Lorn says that until she reaches accountability I can choose my new mentor. And I choose you!"

Maggie began to glow. She was honored and nearly overcome with joy. Generally the regulet assigned a mentee to a curator and it was most often based on merit. Maggie was a fine curator but never thought that her actions would ever merit attention or recognition. She did not expect to be a mentor and to have been chosen by a friend was somehow even more sweet. All at once, however, an idea came to her that completely changed everything.

"Me?" she asked while she continued to ponder this new idea.

"Yes," Dae replied. "Are you pleased?"

"Very pleased," Maggie said. "You said Lorn gave you a choice?"

"That is right," she said.

"Could you make a different choice?" asked Maggie.

A look of confusion broke across Dae's face and her joyful countenance fell.

"Do you not wish to be my mentor?" she asked.

"No, that is not the case at all," Maggie said. "It would be an honor. I only asked because . . . well, never mind. I would love to be your mentor."

"Because what?" Dae pressed. "Why did you ask if I could make a different choice?"

Maggie had counted on Dae's curiosity to overcome her. She knew she would need to proceed delicately, not only to spare her feelings but so that her friend would desire this thing as much as she herself did.

"It was nothing," she began. "Only that I was thinking of Eric and his new friend Lindsey."

"Go on," Dae replied eagerly.

"Well," Maggie continued after a brief pause. "I know that he has feelings for her and I believe she does too, but I spoke with her curator and she was reluctant to speak with me on the subject. I do not fault her for her choice as we are all aware of the counsel."

"Indeed," Dae said.

Maggie let this information hang in the air as she watched Dae's anticipation grow. When she felt the fledgling curator had reached the limits of her anticipation she went on.

"However," she spoke softly.

"Yes," Dae said, almost unconsciously as she leaned closer.

"If her mentee and I were to exchange information I do not see any harm in that," Maggie concluded.

"And who is her mentee?" Dae asked innocently.

Maggie was a bit disappointed that the genius of her plan had not yet sunk in to her young friend. She waited patiently while Dae processed her words. Her face lit up as the realization of Maggie's insinuation came to her.

"Oh, I see," Dae finally said. "I could be her mentee."

Relieved by what appeared to be at least a precursory approval of her plan, Maggie nodded in the affirmative. Almost immediately though Dae looked distraught and Maggie felt her hopes slipping away.

"When I gave my choice to Lorn he headed to the regulet to make the assignment," she said.

"Come, quickly," Maggie urged. "We must see if we can catch him. That is if you are agreeable."

"Oh yes," Dae said. "This is far better than cats and short pants. Come, we must hurry."

They hurried off out of the congreget and down the long hallway that eventually led to the regulet. Dae spotted Lorn immediately by the circular barrier at the center of the grand pavilion.

"There he is," she said to Maggie. "What is the name of her curator?"

"Kya," Maggie answered.

"Right," Dae said. "You stay here and I will go and speak with him."

She began to sail away as Maggie called out to her, "Dae."

She stopped and looked back.

"Thank you," Maggie said.

Dae smiled and quickly turned and continued toward the barrier at the center of the regulet. She approached Lorn who turned to greet her warmly. The two conversed for a moment while Maggie looked on anxiously. Before too long, Lorn turned back to the barrier to speak with someone on the other side and Dae turned back to Maggie with a reassuring smile. Waves of emotions washed over her, relief followed by exhilaration and finally anticipation for the answers she so desired. Her plan had fallen into place; she only hoped now that she and Dae had made the right choice.

Stalker

Eric squinted slightly from the brightness of the sun, which had dropped to the lower portion of the skyline. *Shades. You need to buy some new sunglasses. Or find the old ones.* He walked between two long rows of cars parked perpendicular to a large beige building. Atop the approaching structure was a red sign that read Raley's. This was the same grocery store he had come to every Monday for the past fifty-two weeks. It was exactly half the distance between the office and his apartment so he could pick up everything he would need on the way home. *Peanut butter, bread, orange juice, chicken, potatoes.* Two young men in white shirts and ties emerged through the automatic sliding glass doors and stepped onto the sidewalk. *Mormons. Don't stop.*

Hear them.

The bold white letters appeared on the screen in front of Maggie. Instead of rising up toward her they floated away from her in Eric's direction. She wondered how these promptings registered with Eric. Since they did not emanate from him she was not certain if they were words in his mind or simply impressions. In any case, Eric's quickened pace illustrated that this was a prompting he would not be heeding. *Head down.*

He looked down at the ground and headed straight for the door. *Don't make eye contact. Just get inside the store.* As an involuntary reflex he looked up just as they passed by him. The young man nearest him stopped and smiled. *Crud. You fool. Why did you look up?*

"Hi," the young man said. "I'm Elder Harper." *Keep walking.*

"Hey," Eric said and put his head back down. *Hurry.*

"Do you have a second?" Elder Harper asked. *No. Keep walking.*

"Not really," Eric said as he turned sideways and slid toward the front door. "I'm late to meet somebody." *Liar. Way to go, you lied to a church boy. Straight to hell for you.*

"I understand," he replied with an even bigger smile. *What are you smiling about, dimples?* "We are missionaries for The Christ of Jesus Christ of Latter-days Saints and we share a message of hope and happiness and of our Savior, Jesus Christ. If you are interested give us a call when you have the time." *Nope. Not gonna happen, skippy.*

The missionary with the broad smile handed Eric a small card with a picture of a bearded man in a white robe standing in the clouds surrounded by angels with trumpets. *Don't take it.*

Take the card.

Eric reached back and accepted the card while keeping his momentum moving firmly away.

"Thanks," he muttered. *This is going in the nearest trash. You can't throw away a picture of Jesus. These guys are diabolic.*

"You're welcome," Elder Harper replied. "What was your name?" *Juan Carlos. Don't lie.*

"Eric," he said as the doors slid open and he quickly rounded the corner into the sanctuary of the produce section. *Safe.*

"Nice to meet you, Eric," he heard faintly as the doors slid closed behind him.

Hear them.

They did seem nice. Not interested.

He looked down at the card in his hand. *Heaven. Jesus.* He turned it over and on the back were a telephone number and an address with a tiny picture of a church in the corner. As he retrieved a basket from the top of the red stack beside the door he thoughtfully stared at the card. *I'm good. No need.* After a moment or two he slid the card into his front pocket and looked around to set his course. *Peanut butter.*

At the far end of the store he saw a slender blonde woman standing with her back to him. *April. Carnations. Park. Brad.*

He slowly drifted between the boxes of produce. *Act casual.* He approached the wall of refrigerated vegetables illuminated by the long fluorescent tubes. *Is it her?* With a long intent stare at the piles of green leafy veggies he took quick glances to his right and moved closer to the woman standing in front of the carrots and celery. *Be cool. Don't look.* When she shifted and turned around he quickly looked down and grabbed the nearest bushel in front of him to examine it. *She saw you. Calm down. You're just buying lettuce. There's nothing weird here.* The woman walked out of the produce section and disappeared behind the gondola out of sight. *Don't follow her. Do not follow her.*

Almost unconsciously he placed the green bushel in his basket and walked to the back of the store to the spot he had last seen her. *It's probably not her. What are the odds? Peanut butter. Just go get your peanut butter.* When he arrived at the back of the gondola he looked the length of the store and saw no sign of her. *Gone. It's fine.* He rounded the corner of the first aisle and there she was standing at the opposite end. *Lindsey. Bright eyes. Beautiful.* She held a jar in her hand with the handle of her basket tucked under her arm. Eric immediately turned to face the rack to his right. There were a variety of spices and seasonings, he picked up the first one he saw and turned it over in his hand. *Pretend to read, or really read. Is she looking? Read.* He glanced to his left to find she had vanished. *Gone again. Magician.* With the spice jar still in hand he turned and headed slowly up the aisle. Beyond the row of cans and jars he could see the automatic glass door at the front of the store sliding closed. *Did she just shop lift?* Just then a voice spoke directly behind him.

"Are you a stalker?" the soft voice said. *Ah!*

Heart attack. Eric jumped with a start and turned around to find Lindsey standing directly behind him. The grocery basket rested on her hip and she had a smirk on her face. *So cute. I love her smile. And her lips.* She had her head tilted slightly to the side and her blonde hair hung over her red cotton t-shirt.

"What?" he asked as he tried to compose himself. *Say no.*

"Are you stalking me?" she spoke in a more pronounced fashion. *Kind of. Just say no.*

"No," he answered defensively. *Tell her this is your store. Ask her what SHE is doing here?*

"Really because it looks like you're following me," she said as she moved closer to him and transferred her basket to her free hand. *I was. Don't admit it.*

"I wasn't stalking you," he responded. *The jar. Show her the jar. Change the subject.*

"Are you sure? Because I could swear you were following me." *She's onto you. Just confess.*

"Well I wasn't." *So there.*

"Why? Am I not good enough for you to stalk?" she asked. *What? Where's this going?*

"No, I mean yes," he stammered. "I would totally stalk you." *Slow down, psycho.* "I, uh, I just wasn't stalking you, ya know, right now." *What are you doing? Stop talking!*

"So you are a stalker?" she asked as she failed to contain a smile. *AH! Just run away.*

"I am not a stalker and I was not following you," he said calmly. *Disaster.* "I am just here doing some grocery shopping. That is all." *Hold up the jar.*

He held the jar in his hand at her eye level. She read the label and her smile grew larger. *Oh no. What am I holding?*

"Cumin?" she asked. "You're buying some cumin?" *What's cumin?*

"Yes," he answered coolly and looked down at his basket. *What else do you have? Green leaves.* "I'm making a salad." *Believable.*

"A cumin salad?" she questioned. *Shoot. Is that even a thing? Not believable.*

"Yeah, it's delicious," he added. *What does cumin even taste like? Flee. Just run away.*

She looked down at his basket and her smile broadened even more. *Uh oh.* "You like chard?" she asked. *What's chard?*

Eric looked down at the green leafy contents of his basket at the red and pink stems that were bound together. *Red stems. Is that chard? Give up. This isn't going well.*

"Okay fine," he admitted, unable to suppress a guilty chuckle. "I'm not making a salad. For a second you looked like somebody I know." *April. You are much prettier though. And not pure evil. Beautiful. Bright eyes. Smile.*

"But I am somebody you know," she quipped. *I love this girl. Smart. Quick. So cute.*

"True," he said. "You are. I just didn't expect to see you here at my store." *Crisis averted.*

"This is your store?" she asked playfully. *No. Sort of? Explain.*

"Well I don't own it if that's what you mean," he explained. "But I come here weekly to get groceries and things." *Peanut butter.*

"Things like chard," she laughed. *She owns me and I love it. Flirt.*

"Yes, chard and cumin," he joked. "It's what I live for. Do you come here often?" *Please say yes. Bright eyes. Ask her out. Not to the store, on a date.*

"No, I'm afraid this is my first time," she said. *Offer to show her around. Be smooth.*

"Do you live around here?" *Smooth.*

"I'm not sure I want to disclose that to a stalker." *She is amazing. You'd better get on your game, Eric. Smart and smooth. You got this.*

"That's probably wise," he replied. "Well I live just up the road and, like I said, I come here regularly. So if you like I can give you the grand tour." *Rejection. Please say yes. Don't cry if she says no. Be confident. Smile. Don't be creepy though. Project confidence.*

"That's very kind," she said. "The grand tour sounds lovely." *You are lovely.*

"Great," he said with a broad smile. "You have already found the produce section; I highly recommend the chard by the way, so let's head over to the peanut butter." *Two birds, one stone.*

"Oh," she exclaimed. "From produce to peanut butter, this tour is grand." *She's definitely flirting. You are in. Don't blow it.*

Eric stepped to the side with a deep bow and gestured toward the front of the store. Lindsey walked forward and the two of them moved slowly up the aisle. *Smooth. Smooth like peanut butter. You got this.* A teenage boy in a red apron appeared from around the corner. He set a box on the floor, squatted down and began to empty its contents onto the bottom shelf.

"That's how we do in Sactown," Eric boasted. "Are you from around here?"

"No," she said. "I'm from Redding. I moved here a couple weeks ago." *Redding. North. Trees. River. Camped near Redding when I was six. Pick a talking point.*

"Redding, huh," he said. *Brilliant. Try more words.* "That's on the river, isn't it?"

"Yeah," she answered. *Dead end. Try something else dummy.*

"Well, here on your right you'll find a wide assortment of peanut butter," he began. *Saved by the butter.* "You've got generic, Skippy, Jif, and my personal favorite, Peter Pan."

He picked up a jar with a red label and a yellow lid and proudly displayed it on his forearm like a waiter presenting a bottle of wine. "Are you a creamy or a crunchy girl?" *Say crunchy.*

"I'm actually allergic to peanuts," she replied with a wrinkled up nose. *Fail. Cute face though. You can save this.*

With a graceful twirl he spun around to face the young man in the red apron who had just finished stocking the shelf. The boy stood up with his now empty box and appeared to be startled by Eric's sudden movement.

"My good man," he pronounced with a degree of distinction. *Tone it down.* "Do you sell a peanut butter that does not have any peanuts in it?" *Possibly? Maybe?*

"You mean like butter?" the boy replied. *Drat. No peanuts, no peanut butter.*

"Right," he accepted. *Move on.* "Well we'll put this jar of death back on the shelf and move this tour along." *Nice save.*

Eric led the way to the way around the back to the open area at the store's entrance. They walked between several day-old pastry displays and the numbered aisles. *She smells nice. Ask her what perfume she is wearing. Don't ask her that, weirdo.* He looked down at the multi-colored interwoven bracelet on her right wrist. *Friendship bracelet. Boyfriend? Girlfriend? Best friend?*

"Down Aisle 3 you'll find paper goods, plates, napkins, plastic spoons, dog food, cat food, chew toys and the like," he said as he paused to look at the sign overhead. *Does she have a pet?* "Do you have any pets?" *Please don't say a cat. Cat lady. Or multiple cats. I can live with a dog, but please no cats.*

"No, I'm afraid I don't have any pets," she said. *Thank you!* "I've never really been a pet person." *Me neither.*

"Same," he agreed. "Seems like a lot of time and money to spend on what amounts to a poop machine." *You just said poop!*

Her hair fell across her face as she jerked forward with laughter. *I love her laugh.* She brushed the strands away from her face and tucked them back behind her ear. *That smile. I could look at that smile all day long. You're on a roll, say something else funny.* He continued to walk to the next aisle with Lindsey by his side.

"Speaking of poop," Eric joked. "Down here you'll find various toiletries and hygiene products if you are in need." *Stop saying poop.*

Lindsey recoiled and the expression on her face hardened. *Uh oh.* Eric looked away and began to walk down the aisle with Lindsey lagging behind. *Too far. Come on, doofus.*

"I, uh, I gotta get some soap for cleaning and washing, ya know," he stammered. *Fix this.*

Maggie wished she could do something to help him. All too often when Eric tried to amuse he would stray a bit beyond the realm of good taste. When he was eleven he told four or five jokes in a row at a family picnic and had his cousins doubled over with laughter, even his aunt and uncles chuckled. However, when he ran out of material he tried to make light of his Aunt Clarissa's blouse, comparing it to a circus tent. Maggie was certain she would never forget the horrified look on his mother's face. Eric and Lindsey continued to walk down the row in complete silence. *You're an idiot. Say something.* Eric sheepishly picked up a box of green soap and placed it in his basket.

"Zest fully clean," he said with a forced grin. *Ah. Disaster.*

Lindsey walked on ahead but did not make eye contact. She stopped next to the toilet paper and picked up a package with a cartoon bear on it that read Charmin Ultra. She held it up and looked back at Eric.

"Poop," she said with a high-pitched tone as she wiggled the four pack side-to-side and placed it in her basket. *Awkward. Amazing. So cute.*

A laugh burst from Eric's mouth and all at once they were both smiling and laughing. *She's great. Ask her out.* As quickly as the laughs had come they were gone. Eric walked over to her and they stood eye to eye for a moment. He reached past her and grabbed a four pack of his own and placed it in his basket.

"Don't squeeze the Charmin," he said with a grin. *Cheesy. Clichéd. You're better than that.*

They stood and stared at each other smiling. *Don't let this moment pass. Her smile. Her eyes. Stay here forever.* She looked away up the aisle and Eric followed her gaze. He turned and headed slowly toward the back of the store.

"I like to cut down here to get milk, meat, and cheese," he said as the tour continued. "What's your favorite kind of milk?" *What a weird question? Chocolate.*

"Um, skim milk I guess," she answered. *Skim milk? No.*

"The correct answer was chocolate," he joked. *Now I want chocolate milk.*

She giggled as she pulled open the glass door and retrieved a carton of skim milk. *That laugh. Make her laugh again.*

"Ron Swanson says that skim milk is water lying about being milk," he added with a big grin. *That's good stuff.*

"Who's Ron Swanson?" *Oh my goodness I have so much to teach this girl.*

"Ron Swanson," he repeated with a knowing tone. "He's Ron Swanson, the greatest character in television history. Actually, he's just Nick Offerman being Nick Offerman but it's brilliant. You've never seen Parks and Rec?" *First Star Wars and now this.*

"I don't own a TV," she added. *No TV? Yikes!*

"No TV?" he exclaimed as he continued out of the dairy section. "What do you do for entertainment?" *Easy, or she'll think you're dumb. Too late.*

"I read, mostly," Lindsey explained. "And I write poetry." *Poetry. Oh boy. This is going sideways. Poetry? She definitely thinks you're dumb, TV boy.*

"That's cool," Eric replied. *Say something smarter.* He stopped and pulled open the glass door to an adjoining refrigerator. Condensation instantly formed and froze on the glass. *Poetry. Tell her about your dad. Too soon. Don't talk about your family.* He looked inside and found the desired red and orange carton. *Donald Duck. No pulp.* He quickly placed it in his basket and let the heavy door swing shut.

"Donald Duck, huh?" she questioned. *Yeah buddy.*

"Oh yeah," he said enthusiastically. "It's the best. You like OJ?" *The juice not the murderer.*

"Sure," she replied. *Invite her over for orange juice. That's weird, right?*

"Well right this way to the deli," he said. *Abrupt transition. Come on, Eric. Be smooth.* They walked past a counter with a variety of meats and cheeses. *I love that smell.* Maggie imagined what all the different colored meats must smell like. She could not wait to taste food but only because she knew nothing about it. It was just one of the aspects of mortality that fascinated her. *Is she a vegetarian?*

"Do you eat meat?" Eric asked. *If she says no just walk away.*

"Yeah," she answered. *Thank you!* "Chicken, turkey, beef, bacon, I eat it all." *Yes! Bacon.*

"I love bacon!" he exclaimed.

"Who doesn't?" she answered. *Marry me.*

"What are your thoughts on turkey bacon?" he probed. *This is the real test.*

"Not a fan," she replied. *Bingo.*

"It's an abomination, right?" he said excitedly. *Too strong. Back it down.*

"There's definitely something wrong with it," she chuckled. *Ask her out.*

"Well, all this bacon talk is making me hungry," Eric said. "I guess I'll have to get some."

He reached into to the pork belly display and picked up a package of Oscar Meyer bacon. *Ask her if she wants some. She can come over for bacon and orange juice. Wait, those are breakfast foods, she might get the wrong idea . . . or the right one, meow. Lock it down, Eric.* He placed the bacon in his basket next to the Donald Duck orange juice, on top of the bushel of chard. *What am I going to do with that?* Lindsey also reached over and snatched a package of bacon. *There goes my bacon invite.*

"Our next stop is the frozen food section," he declared as they moved on. *Ice cream.*

They walked side by side down the aisle, flanked by large refrigerated cabinets. *Chicken. Ice cream. Stir fry. Pizza.* "On the left are your frozen treats, ice cream, frozen yogurt, sherbet and a variety of ice cream related items," he said with a sweeping gesture. "And on your right is where I live, frozen foods."

"Do you cook?" she asked. *Not really. Is that a problem?*

"Does heating up a frozen pizza count?" he asked timidly. *Dave cooks. I heat.*

"No." *Drat.*

"Then no." *I flip omelets like a pro. Stop with the breakfast insinuations.*

With an amused look on her face she surveyed the items on the frozen food side. *Oh man, she thinks I'm a loser.* He walked behind her a few steps until he saw a bag of boneless skinless chicken. *That's got to count.* He quickly opened the door, pulled out a bag and held it in the air.

"I grill a mean chicken though," he proclaimed. "How about that?" *Be impressed.*

"Are you asking if that counts or if I want grilled chicken?" Lindsey questioned.

"If it counts," he replied. *NO! You idiot! That was your window. Ask her if she wants grilled chicken. AHHH!*

"I suppose that counts," she said with a hint of disappointment. *You blew it. Moment gone.*

She continued up the aisle looking blankly into the glass cabinets. Eric followed after her with his head down. *Fool. It was right there in front of you. Too late.* At the end of the row was a wide, open section with breads, rolls, pastries, donuts, and cookies. In the far corner was a shelf full of dark wine bottles. *Does she drink? Probably best not to bring it up unless you plan to start. Let's just get this over with.*

"We have arrived in the bakery," he announced. "I recommend the whole wheat bread, it's delicious." *There, maybe she'll think you are healthy. Don't look at the donuts.*

"Well, with your recommendation, I shall have to try it," she said with a faux sophistication. *Cute. She's still in, I think.*

They stood in front of a lighted shelf full of bread. After a moment or two they each picked out a loaf of bread and placed it atop the items in their baskets. *Oh no. This is it. Think of something. Stall. Mention the donuts. No, don't. Ah. What are you going to do? Ask her out, you coward.*

"The final stop on our tour is the checkout, where you will meet the most delightfully friendly checkers in the business," he said and once more stepped to the side with a grand gesture for her to proceed back to the front of the store. *It's over. Too fast. How did this go so fast?*

"Did you get everything you were after?" he asked. *Say no and we'll stay here forever.*

"Almost," she replied. *Almost?*

"What else did you need? I'm sure we can find it," he said earnestly. *Anything. Name it.*

"No, no," she said. "It's nothing. I, I, maybe I'll find it later." *She just wants to get away from you psycho. You messed up.*

Maggie was desperate to know what Lindsey was thinking. She believed she knew what it was that she was not saying and could not wait to speak with Dae about it. They walked in silence to the register. *Be a gentleman.*

"After you," he said. *Chivalry.*

Lindsey stepped forward and placed the items in her basket on the black conveyor belt. They gently slid towards the plump woman behind the counter. She had a round face and wore a red apron that complemented her beautiful brown skin. Her black curls bounced atop her head as she slid Lindsey's purchases across the scanner. The nametag on her apron read "Chanel" in bold white letters. Eric began to unload his basket just as the checker picked up the last of Lindsey's groceries.

"Are you two together, sugar?" the woman asked. *If only.*

"No," Lindsey replied. "We're separate." *Separate. Ouch. It's true but it still sounded harsh.*

"That'll be $20.15," the woman said. *Offer to pay. Too soon? Too much?*

Lindsey pulled a wallet from her purse and handed over a twenty-dollar bill. She fiddled for another moment for some loose change at the bottom of her purse before retrieving two coins and paying for her groceries. *This is it. Man up.* Finally, she took hold of two plastic bags and turned back toward Eric. *Now or never.*

"Well, thanks for the tour," she said and began to turn toward the exit. *Wait!*

"Wait!" Eric blurted out. *That was loud. You're going to frighten her. Control yourself.* "Uh, Lindsey, would you . . . ? Would you like to go out on a date? With me?" *Oh boy. No turning back now.*

"I'd like that," she said with a smile. *WOOWHOO! Stay calm. Be cool.*

"Cool," Eric replied casually. "I'll, um, I'll see you tomorrow then." *No plan. She said yes though. Good enough. Make a plan tonight.*

"I'll see you tomorrow," she said. She smiled at Eric and then over at Chanel. After a moment she turned and walked out the front door. Eric watched until the doors slid closed behind her. When he turned back toward the register he saw that Chanel watched him with amusement. *What's her deal?*

"Real smooth, sugar," she said in a mocking tone. "Real smooth." *Maybe not, but it got the job done. Mission accomplished. Now I just have to plan an amazing date and not throw up or embarrass myself. No problem.*

The Other Side

There were precious few spirits in the congreget when Maggie arrived. As soon as Eric had fallen asleep she filed his last few conscious thoughts, which had been of Lindsey, and flew from the box. When she did not immediately see Dae she settled in next to an open platform and watched the multitude grow with each arrival. All attempts at distraction failed as her overwhelming desire was to exchange perspectives with her friend. She knew how her beholden felt about Lindsey, but without the knowledge Dae was privy to, she could not be entirely sure how she felt for him.

At last a large group of spirits entered the congreget, among them was Dae and her new mentor, Kya. Maggie started to go to them on impulse but halted when she remembered how reluctant Kya had been to share Lindsey's thoughts with her. She swayed side-to-side in a vain attempt to draw Dae's attention. They joined with another group of curators and were in the midst of a joyous exchange when Dae finally looked around the congreget. She smiled when she saw Maggie and nodded. Maggie returned her smile and tried to will Dae to her. When that failed she chose to be patient and wait for her to break away from the group. Each moment that passed was agonizing. Dae appeared to be the center of the discussion with her newfound friends. Had Dae forgotten their agreement so soon? Or had Maggie been cast aside by these new acquaintances? Did Kya seek to sabotage their plans by keeping Dae from her? Finally Dae excused herself and sailed to Maggie.

"Salutations, Maggie," she greeted her warmly.

"Salutations," Maggie replied. "Well?"

"She likes him very much," Dae reported.

Maggie began to glow. "I knew it. I am so pleased."

Dae looked anxiously over her shoulder to the group she had just left. Maggie followed her gaze and was met with the beaming stare of Dae's mentor, Kya. Maggie simply met her displeasure with a smile and a nod. Dae turned back to Maggie and looked down toward the platform beside them.

"Do not worry about her," Maggie said. "There is no harm in this."

"Maggie," Dae began. "I think there might be. We have been counseled against such an exchange and His counsel is wise. If there was no danger, there would be no need for counsel."

"Danger, yes," Maggie conceded. "But not harmful. We will be cautious. Our intentions are good. We can share what we know and remain as we are now. This will not change the job we have to do. Besides, you are a mentee, this is not your beholden, and so we are safe. You need not worry."

"We will be cautious?" she queried.

"Very cautious," Maggie assured her.

"Very well," Dae said. "If we feel we are nearing danger then we will cease our exchange."

"Most definitely," Maggie agreed.

She would have agreed to almost any terms at this point. Her desire to learn the other side of their exchange nearly caused her to burst. She had to restrain herself so as to not frighten her young accomplice. However, despite Dae's reserved speech and sensible nature, she was just as keen to share as Maggie was.

"Where shall I begin?" Dae asked.

"From the start of course," Maggie replied with glee.

"Well, she spotted him as soon as he entered the store," Dae began with great enthusiasm. "She wondered if he would notice her and if he would remember her."

"What a strange fear," Maggie interrupted. "They had just spoken days previous."

"Maggie, she has so much doubt," Dae explained. "The things she tells herself at times are harrowing."

Maggie recalled the times when Eric would get down on himself. In those dark times negativity swept over him in waves and he felt of little worth. The adversary had great influence in the finite world and he lay in constant wait to seize hold of those he could. Those were moments she prayed would pass quickly. She thought of Borador and the depths he had witnessed with not one but two waywards and could easily empathize with his choice to withdraw. She momentarily wondered when he might appear in the congreget and join them.

"When did she realize that he saw her?" she asked.

"When he appeared at the end of the row she was certain," Dae responded. "She dashed around the corner and circled behind him. Maggie, she was so terrified but she forced herself to take a risk. She thought that if she could do this one thing that her mother would be proud of her. She thinks of her mother a lot."

"Eric had doubts as well," Maggie interjected. "His thoughts were focused on his missteps and where he had gone wrong. He even told untruths at first."

"She suspected that he was being untruthful with his claims and did not believe there was a cumin salad or that he would eat such a thing," Dae said.

"Was she upset at his dishonesty?" Maggie asked.

"No," Dae answered. "She seemed to delight in his attempts to deceive."

"How strange."

"Yes," Dae continued. "Especially considering that many of her doubts originate from the hurt caused by the dishonesty of others."

"But she likes Eric?" Maggie questioned again.

"Oh yes, very much," Dae said. "Cute was the thought most prevalent in her mind during their encounter."

"He finds her cute as well," Maggie said. She wondered what exactly cute was and what they found cute about each other. They were very different in the nature and even more different in their appearance. Their words and thoughts differed as well yet they both used the same adjective for the other. She questioned her basic understanding of a word that could be used so broadly.

"She was so grateful for his invitation to show her around the store," Dae said.

"He was relieved she accepted," said Maggie.

"Did he find her peanut allergy to be disappointing?" Dae asked. "Lindsey is worried it will be seen as a disadvantage."

"Not at all," Maggie said. "He was much more concerned with it making her uncomfortable than anything else."

"I am happy to know that he is considerate," Dae said. "Lindsey is sensitive and deserves someone with a kind heart."

Maggie was pleased to hear that Dae thought well of Eric. She maintained that even though he struggled through the past year that he had not lost his goodness, he simply turned his focus toward the things which brought him down. Her hope now was that Lindsey would help to restore him to his former self.

"He does have a kind heart," Maggie concurred. "Although sometimes his words are unbridled and at times can be offensive."

Dae giggled. "I know of that which you are speaking."

"His reference to bodily waste?"

"Indeed," she answered with a smile.

"Did Lindsey take offense?"

"She was shocked, yes," Dae explained. "But it quickly turned to amusement. I cannot tell if that was due to the subject matter or his discomfort afterwards."

"In either case I am relieved," Maggie said. "His humor is often beyond the bounds of good taste."

"Well she found him very humorous," Dae said. "From what I can tell it is what she likes best about him. She does not regularly have cause to laugh and she so needs it. Do you find Eric amusing?"

"He has his moments," Maggie said with a smile. She recalled the occasions when his thoughts or his words had given her cause to laugh. In most cases the things that he thought were of far greater entertainment than the things that he said. She did not believe that any finite could know him as well as she did.

"She also worries that she does not know enough about the television shows and movies that he speaks of," Dae shared.

"And he worries that she will find him unintelligent or uninteresting because he does not read as she does," Maggie replied.

"It appears they both harbor fears that could easily be dispelled if they shared them with each other," Dae observed.

"What you say is true but that is the way with finites," Maggie explained. "They do not speak their fears for fear of how it might be received and thus their fear breeds fear. When they become more familiar with one another, over time, they come to trust in each other. Only with trust do they allow themselves to be vulnerable, which casts off fear and brings a closeness that is both dangerous and safe at the same time."

"That sounds wonderful," Dae said.

"It can be," Maggie said. "But if that trust is broken there is great pain. And the fear returns tenfold. After that it is much more difficult to trust again."

She had seen Eric go through this cycle many times in his life in varying degrees. It was most common with females who he had a great desire to be close with. This last time had been the worst. His trust was so complete that the pain was almost unbearable for him when it was broken. His thoughts seemed to suffocate him in the days and weeks that followed. He hardly left his apartment and was consumed with bitterness and resentment. Maggie worried he might never recover, but that was before Lindsey. With her, Maggie had new hope.

"Lindsey must have been hurt very badly then," said Dae. "She is beset by fear and pain nearly every waking moment. Her encounter with Eric was the lone bright spot in her day."

"I am saddened to learn of her pain," Maggie said and her countenance dimmed.

"Yes," Dae added. "It is sad."

They were silent for a time. Dae stared blankly at the white floor beneath them and Maggie peered right through her at the room beyond. She considered Eric and his experiences and wondered what travails Lindsey might have suffered. All at once Borador came into her consciousness. She looked around the congreget but he was nowhere to be found. Her impulse was to seek him out but she did not know where to start.

"Maggie?" Dae said, breaking the silence.

"Yes, my dove," Maggie answered almost unconsciously as she woke from her brief stupor.

"What do you think it is like to eat?" she asked.

Maggie had wondered this many times before. She had observed closely how it was done and the thoughts that it induced. Eric thought about it many times a day. He began thinking of his next meal hours before it was to come and not long after he had just eaten. She imagined it must be a wonderful experience for all the energy the finites devoted to it.

"I do not know," Maggie replied. "Why do you ask?"

"No reason," she said. "I am just curious about bacon. Vila said that nothing was more universally loved by the finites than bacon. Thelma loved it. Lindsey loves it. Eric said he did. Do you think there's bacon in N'Djamena?"

"I do not know, Eric has not traveled far from home." Maggie answered. "So Lindsey truly loves bacon?"

"Oh yes, very much," Dae said. "She was pleased Eric agreed."

"Eric was more than pleased," she said. "He wished to marry her on the spot."

"Oh Maggie," Dae beamed. "Do you think they will get married?"

"It is far too early to tell," Maggie said. "Let us see how their first date goes."

"Yes, the date," Dae agreed. "What are his plans?"

"He was still formulating his plans as he drifted off to sleep," Maggie said. "His last thoughts were of miniature golf and pizza."

"Oh that would be lovely," Dae said. "I am sure they will have a delightful time."

"Let us hope so," Maggie said. She looked around the congreget again. "Have you seen Borador?"

"No," said Dae. "I have not. Where do you suppose he is?"

"I do not know," Maggie said with a tone of worry. In her search for Borador she noticed that Kya had broken off from her group and was making her way toward them. Dae looked nervously back toward Maggie.

"Salutations," Kya said to Maggie.

"Salutations," Maggie responded.

Kya turned to Dae and waited for her acknowledgement. Dae slowly turned away from Maggie to look into the solemn face of her mentor. "Dae, you should come and join us. We are discussing the distinction between aspirational thoughts and motivational thoughts. It would be of great worth for you to hear."

"Oh," Dae said with a glance toward Maggie. "Yes, I would be interested of course, but I am communing with my friend."

"She can come as well," Kya suggested. "An appropriate information exchange is one that is beneficial for all."

She turned to Maggie. They stared at each other for a moment with Dae caught between them like a planet orbited by dueling moons. Despite her pleasant demeanor, it was clear that Kya was firm in her commitment to bring an end to their consorting. She waited with an unyielding patience for one or both of them to acquiesce. Maggie did not wish to give in but was unwilling to be the source of contention.

"I would be happy to join your discussion," Maggie finally said. "Perhaps we can provide a fresh perspective."

"Or perhaps you might be enlightened through proper discourse," Kya said.

"We can only hope," Maggie replied.

The trio headed off toward the larger group with Kya in front, followed by an anxious Dae and finally by Maggie. She worried that she had put Dae in a difficult position with her new mentor. In her haste to seek out her objective, she had hardly considered the consequences Dae might face. Maggie repented and vowed that she would set things as they should be for Dae's sake. Besides, she had learned all she wanted to know. Lindsey thought well of Eric and she was the hope that Maggie had been seeking. She was a bright spot in his life and he in hers. Whatever the future held, at least for the time being, all was well.

Milestone

I'm just saying, he was honoring his father," Mark said. *By letting him die?*

"By letting him getting sucked up in a cyclone?" Eric shouted. *That's insane.*

"He didn't want anyone to discover what he was capable of," Mark argued. *But why?*

"Who?" Eric asked. "The six people cowering beneath the underpass?" *That makes no sense. He died because he was stupid. Clark should have saved him.*

"It makes sense when you think about who he is," Mark rebutted. *He's freaking Superman!*

"He's freaking Superman!" Eric said, raising his voice again. "He's freaking Superman and Superman saves people. He would certainly have saved his father. And he wouldn't go around snapping necks either." *Freaking Zach Snyder. Man of Kill.*

"Look," Mark interrupted. "It was a great movie. Those fight scenes were off the chain." *Don't say off the chain. Too old.*

"I didn't say it was a bad movie, I said it was a bad Superman movie," Eric argued. *There's a difference. And S doesn't stand for hope, it stands for freaking Superman.*

Although she executed her tasks with her usual precision and speed, Maggie could not help but be bored with his current conversation. She had lost track of the inconsequential thoughts that sprang to Eric's mind while he argued with his coworker about the details of a film. What she found interesting was that there was a sharp decline in critical or analytical thoughts while he watched movies or television. Those thoughts generally came after the fact when he was free from the visual onslaught and had time to reflect.

She wished that he would devote the same time and energy into other, more worthwhile pursuits, but those were not the things that interested him.

"So you want to put Superman back in red underpants?" Mark asked. *Yes. Kind of. No, not really. Christopher Reeves.*

"Maybe," Eric lied. "Whatever he wears he should, oh I don't know, save somebody, you know, instead of murdering the last of his kind." *Neck snap. Horrible.*

"Would you rather he flew around the world super-fast to reverse time?" asked Mark. *Ouch.*

"No," Eric grumpily conceded. *That was bad.* "All I'm saying is that we were missing a little truth, justice, and the American way." *Stink'n Brit. Cast an American.*

"*Man of Steel* was better than the Dick Donner Superman movies in every way," Mark declared. *What? WHAT?*

"You are insane!" Eric shouted. *Crazy. What an idiot.*

"Better effects, better costume, better story, better cast, better score," Mark continued. *Christopher Reeves. Don't let that stand.*

"Hold on right there," Eric interrupted and stood up out of his chair. "I'll give you the effects and slight nod to the costume and story. I'll even lean ever so slightly to the score, which was amazing, but if you disrespect Chris Reeves again I'll punch you in the mouth." *Justice served.*

"Fine," Mark said. "So you're saying that *Man of Steel* is better in every way except Christopher Reeves." *Trapped! How did this happen? You're smarter than this. I hate this guy. Just punch him.*

Eric sat back down in his chair with his mouth agape and stared at his coworker. *Save your father. Neck snap. IHOP.* The vain in his forehead throbbed and pulsed. *So angry. Yell something at him. Not a Superman movie. Muted colors. AH!* He shifted uncomfortably in his seat as Mark smiled back at him calmly. *Pull his mustache and poke him in the eye. Three Stooges.* The back office door swung open and Bill stepped through the threshold.

"When you two nerds are done with your slap fight, I need one of you to install Project on the new admin's system," Bill said. *Lindsey. Bright eyes. Mine.*

"I'll do it," Mark said. *What? No way!* He stood up and walked toward the software rack. Eric leapt from his chair and blocked his path. *Back off buddy.*

"I've got it," Eric said. *Establish dominance.* He locked eyes with Mark, squinted and clenched his jaw. *Look tough.*

"Easy, fella," Mark said as he stepped away from Eric with his hands raised in surrender. "You go for it." *Calm down, Eric. You went a little too far. Breathe. Be gracious.*

"Thank you," Eric said. *Be casual.* "I was heading out anyway so I'll just take care of it while I'm at it." *Nice cover.*

"Uh huh," Mark said skeptically.

Eric walked over to the small silver rack that was lined with clear plastic cases. *Project. Project. Where's Project?* After a brief survey of the top row he reached out and pulled one of the cases forward with his index finger. *MS Project. Got it.* With the disc in hand he turned around and headed for the door. He turned his head slightly to see Bill and Mark watching him with amusement. *What are they looking at?*

"What?" Eric questioned. *You both look ridiculous. Stupid grins.*

"You like her," Mark said. *Shut up.* Bill chuckled and smiles broke across both their faces.

"I'm just doing my job," Eric tried to deflect the assertion. *And, yes I like her.* "You should try it." *Take that.*

Bill and Mark began laughing. Eric pulled open the door aggressively. *Jerks.* He turned back to his coworkers and opened his mouth. *Bullies. Jerks. Duty Heads. Don't call them Duty Heads.* Mark, who was nearly doubled over with laughter, wiped a tear away from his eye and Bill went back into his office. *They're not worth it.* Without another word Eric exited the room and the door closed behind him. He could still hear Mark's muted laughter through the door. *Ugh. What a clown.*

"Hey there," a soft voice called from down the hall. *Bright Eyes.*

He turned toward the sound of the voice to see Lindsey heading in his direction. She wore a bright yellow sweater and khaki slacks. *Wow.* Her golden locks bounced as she walked and she smiled brightly at him. *Gorgeous.* He leaned back against the door and greeted her with a half wave. *Be cool. Be funny.*

"Hey girl," he said playfully. *What was that? Hey girl? Come on, man. Guess it's better than Hey'll.*

She laughed and reached up to push a lock of hair away from her face. Eric noticed that she was carrying a jug of water in her arms.

Help her.

The white words appeared on the screen in front of Maggie. She looked beyond the impression in front of her and watched eagerly to see what Eric would do.

"Let me help you with that," he offered. *Chivalry.*

"That's okay," she replied. "I've got it." *Women's lib. Let her carry it. She doesn't want your help. Do it anyway. She might get mad.*

"I insist," said Eric. He placed the plastic case in his pocket and took the jug from her as she drew near. *She's so pretty.*

"Thank you," she said. *You are welcome. And beautiful. Tell her she's beautiful. No, don't. That's creepy.*

"No problem," he said. They walked up the hallway side by side. "I was headed your way anyway."

"You were?" she asked. She tilted her head sideways and grinned. *Tell her you wanted to see her. But don't make it creepy.*

"Yeah, you need Project installed on your PC," he replied. *Coward.*

"Oh yes," she said. "Project."

Her words trailed off and she folded her arms and looked up the hall. *She sounds disappointed. Tell her you wanted to see her.* They walked in silence out through the cubicles. When they reached the end of the row they turned right and passed a small cubby with some cupboards and a sink. *Sink. Water. Jug.*

"You know you could fill this up in there so you don't have to walk so far," Eric suggested.

"It's for his coffee maker and Leonard wants me to use filtered water," she responded. *Stalin. Of course he does. What a jerk.*

"Oh," Eric replied. *Say something besides "Oh." Come on, genius.*

They turned right again and headed down Executive Row. A low hum could be heard from the muffled voices in the cubicles. Eric peered in to the first cube and saw Janice talking on the phone. She looked up and smiled at him. *Smile back.* He nodded with a smile as they moved beyond the cubicle wall and she passed out of sight. Ahead, to their left, the door to Leonard Salmen's office was open. There was a lone lamp in the dimly lit office and the chair behind the desk was unoccupied. *He's not in there. Thank goodness.*

"Hey, congratulations," Eric said with a smile. *You're still here.*

"For what," she asked. *You made it.*

"It's been a week and you're still here," replied Eric. "Trust me, that is an accomplishment." *Little Stalin.* He gestured toward the office door. Lindsey turned and glanced over her shoulder. She chuckled nervously and looked back to Eric.

"Thanks, I'll take it from here," Lindsey said as she reached out and took the jug back from Eric. The back of her hand brushed up against his chest. *Flex.* Eric tensed up. *But look natural.*

"No problem," he replied. "I'll just slip in here and get your install started." *She touched me. Keep it together.*

Lindsey smiled and nodded before she turned and walked into the open office. Eric watched her carry the jug over to the credenza and placed it next to a black and chrome coffee maker. *Bet that costs more than she makes in a week. Nice slacks. She fills out those slacks nicely. No. Creeper. Don't be that guy. Install. Install the software. Forgive me.* He slipped into his tiny cubicle and sat down in the black swivel chair. *This is where she sits. She's touched this chair. What is your deal? Get it together!*

Maggie filed each thought in the category they belonged to. Some were tagged as base thoughts while others were tagged as complimentary and still others as directive action. She had long contemplated the base response of a male to the lines and curves of the female anatomy. Without exception they triggered an onslaught of thoughts in all varieties. Often Eric dismissed them or attempted to bring them up from their base nature but occasionally he let them linger and gave in to the baseness of his nature. Maggie was thankful that this was not one of those times. She noticed that there was a direct correlation between the esteem he felt for the female and the brevity of his baseness.

Eric pressed a button on the front of the computer beneath the monitor and a small shelf slid open. Several pink post-it notes hung from the monitor with individual doodles. *She's an artist.* One was of a flower with five petals; next to it was a looping heart-shaped design that sat atop a tripod. There were little sketches of trees, a diapered cherub with a bow and arrow, and a sun wearing sun-glasses. He removed a shiny silver disc from the case and placed it on the shelf. Gently, he pushed the shelf back into the black box and peered over the half wall counter to look into the office across the hall. *She looks so nice today.* Lindsey was still busy at work next to the coffee maker. She poured the jug into a container beside the chrome and black machine. *Tell her she looks nice. That's not creepy, right? Girls like that. Better be safe.* Eric reached blindly to the right of the keyboard and touched the desk with his fingers. He felt around for a moment and looked down when his hand found nothing but a box of tissues. *Where's the mouse?* Where he expected to find the mouse there was a post-it pad with a scribbled out drawing on top. He looked closely at what appeared to be a noose that had been marked over with multiple zigzagged lines. *That's not sunshine and flowers, is it?* He scanned the top of the desk until he found what he was looking for on the opposite side of the keyboard. *She's left-handed. That's cool.*

"You're left-handed?" Eric questioned. *Was that too loud?*

Lindsey walked out of the office with an empty water jug.

"What's that?" she asked. *Repeat the question.*

"You are left-handed," he said. *That wasn't a question. She's so pretty.*

"Yep," she said. "I sure am. Are you left-handed?" *No. I wish I was now, though.*

"No," he replied. "That means your artistic, right?" *Is that true? Don't just say stuff, you'll sound dumb. She already thinks your dumb, movie boy.*

"I don't think that's necessarily true," said Lindsey. "I mostly doodle. I do like to write, though. Does that count as artistic?" *She draws, reads, and writes. What do you do? Play video games and eat. You need to expand your interests. Skydiving? Nah, too dangerous.*

"It does to me," he said. "What do you write?" *Poetry, remember? Dad.*

"Poetry," she said. *I still got nothing. Say something that rhymes.*

"That's cool," replied Eric. *Nothing. No poems. You uncultured swine.*

Lindsey placed the jug on the counter and leaned over the half wall to see her monitor. Eric immediately turned his attention to the task at hand. *Look hard working.* With an intense stare he studied the windows open on her desktop. He clicked through the prompts in a rhythmic fashion. *No mistakes. She's watching. Time to impress.* He keyed in the numerical code printed on the inside of the case on a black and white label. A green status bar appeared on the screen and grew longer, left to right. In a few moments a button appeared that read "Complete." Eric moved the mouse and clicked the button. *Done.*

"All set," he declared. He pressed the button on the front of the computer and retrieved the disc from the tray before gently pushing it closed. The new icon on her desktop was nearly camouflaged by the greens in the wood pictured background wallpaper. *Forest. Camping. Redding? Home.* He rolled the chair away from her workstation and stood up. "Is that Redding?"

Lindsey walked around the pillar and joined Eric in the small cubicle. "The trees?"

"Yeah," Eric said with a gesture to the monitor. *She smells nice.*

"No," she replied. "It's just a background from the Internet." *That was a bust.*

"Oh," he said. "Do you miss it?"

"Redding?" *No, trees. Yes, Redding.*

"Yeah." *Small talk. Make small talk.*

"Not really," she said. *Dead end. This is painful.*

"Is your family still up there?" *Family. Good call. Talk about family.*

"Yes," she said with a tone of melancholy. She looked away at the corner of her cube. *Is she sad? Does she miss them? What is she thinking? Did I touch a nerve? Change the subject.*

"Do you miss them?" *That's not changing the subject, doofus.*

"No," she said flatly. *And that's that. It's over. Super job, Eric.*

"Um, well I'd better get back to work," Eric said. He slipped around the column and out into the hall. "I'll see you later." *Hopefully.*

"No, wait," Lindsey said. *Yes, ma'am.*

Eric stopped at the counter and looked over the half wall into the cubicle where Lindsey was still standing. She looked at him for a moment with big, glistening eyes. *Is she going to cry? Please don't cry.* Lindsey plopped down in her chair and put her face in her hands. *What's happening? She's definitely going to cry. Shoot. Do something, Eric.*

"I'm sorry," she said earnestly as she looked up and forced a smile. *Sorry for what?*

"Don't be," said Eric. "I was too pushy." *Way to go.*

"No, you weren't," said Lindsey. "It's just . . ."

Her words drifted into the air and a far off look fell on her face. *Just what? Hello? What is she thinking? Be patient.* Maggie felt Eric's impatience as she too burned to know what was on Lindsey's mind. She imagined what Dae must be seeing and hearing and looked forward to their meetings in the congreget. She remembered her vow and reasoned that one last exchange would not do them any harm. Eric leaned over the counter and watched intently. *It's okay, I'm here.*

". . . it's just," she went on. "It's difficult to talk about it. Things were not good for me at home. It's why I'm here." *Sounds heavy. What can I do?*

"I'm sorry," he said. *Offer a hug. Would that be creepy?*

"Please, please don't feel sorry for me!" she shot back. *Whoah. That was intense.*

"Sorr . . ." Eric caught himself. "I mean, that's unfortunate." *Just run away.*

"Do not run," Maggie said aloud. *Do not run.* The thought popped up on the screen and sounded into the box like an echo, only in Eric's voice. Maggie wondered again if she had made that happen. She was behind the platform and a safe distance from the portal. Had she put that thought into Eric's mind? She replayed the warnings and counsel she had received and feared she was becoming too involved. Still, no harm was done and she simply resolved not to let it happen again.

Eric and Lindsey both looked away in opposite directions. The silenced filled the air. *What now?* Eric fidgeted nervously while Lindsey sat as still as a statue in her chair.

"And that's that," she whispered. *What's that?*

"What?" Eric asked.

"You were bound to find out eventually," she replied. "I'm a mess. I understand if you don't want to go out any more." *No.*

"Are you kidding me?" he asked. *Where did that come from?* "Everybody's got a messed-up family. I come from toothless, barefoot hillbillies; literally, they have no teeth. Well, except for Uncle Ern, he's got one chomper up front that he calls his bottle opener." *Too much?*

Lindsey laughed. *Oh, that laugh. More please.* Her smile faded and she wiped a fledgling tear from her eye. *Hug her.*

"Eric, I'm serious," she said as she straightened herself up in her chair. "I'm damaged. You don't want to be around me." *Oh, but I do.*

"We're all damaged, a little," he argued. *Or in Uncle Ern's case, a lot.*

"Not like this," she said. "Not like me." *Who hurt you? Hug her. Tell her how you feel.*

"Damaged or not, I like you," he began. "I like to be near you, I like to talk with you. I want to know you, the good and the bad." *I want to wipe away your tears. I want to hold you. I want to hurt whoever hurt you. I want to make you smile.*

"You won't like what you find," she said. *I doubt that.*

"I don't believe that," he said. "Even so, I'd like to find out for myself. Besides, if you don't go out with me, you'll never meet Uncle Ern and you know you're dying to see the chomper."

She laughed again and this time her smile did not fade. *You did it. Keep it up.*

"This Thursday," said Eric. "Let's go out this Thursday." *Confidence.*

"Thursday?" she questioned. *You bet.*

"Yes, because I don't want to wait for the weekend," he declared. *Deal with it. Say yes.*

She nodded vigorously. *Was that a yes?*

"Yeah?" he asked hopefully.

"Yeah." *Woowhoo!*

"Hey!" a deep voice thundered from up the hall. Eric turned to see Leonard Salmen bearing down on him. *Stalin. Jerk. Animal.* "What are you doing here?"

Eric turned to face him as the burly bullish brute stopped just short of making physical contact with him. *What is that smell? Too much cologne. I hate this guy.* Salmen glowered at him from behind his well-groomed mustache. His dark beady eyes assaulted Eric's face. *Don't back down.* Eric straightened up and tried to make himself taller.

"I was just installing some software," Eric stated and held up the CD case. *Back off, jerk.*

"I bet you were," Salmen insinuated. *What does that mean?*

"He was putting Project on my PC," Lindsey offered. *I got this, Lindsey.*

"I don't care what you call it," Salmen bellowed. "This isn't a nightclub. It's a place of business. She has work to do." *What is your problem?*

Eric drew in a deep breath and furloughed his brow. Salmen leaned in and clinched his jaw. *Bring it, garlic breath.*

"He's finished," Lindsey said. "He was just leaving." *I was not.*

Eric looked over at Lindsey. She offered a nervous grin and a reassuring nod. *Fine.*

"Yep," he added. "Just leaving." *You're lucky, Stalin.*

Salmen did not move as Eric turned to leave. They bumped shoulders and Eric was temporarily knocked off balance. *Freaking jerk. Ugh. Don't turn around.* He glanced into Janice's cubicle as he passed it and she gave him a pitiful look. *Eavesdropper.* Eric turned the corner and heard Salmen's grating and garbled voice. *Monster. I hope she's okay.*

Apart

She was more anxious than ever to depart once he had fallen asleep. The moment his thoughts for the day had been filed and uploaded, she exited the box and started down the hallway to gather with the other curators. While she was certain there would be a good number of spirits socializing and studying in the congreget, she was only concerned with one. Dae was one of two souls in the department with access to the knowledge she desired and she was grateful for her willingness to share.

As she approached the entrance, however, her purpose melted away in an instance at an unexpected sight. Borador emerged into the hallway just beyond a multitude of other spirits who were leaving their respective boxes. He turned and headed away from the congreget while all others made their way through the large archway where Maggie was headed.

"Borador," she called after him.

He did not look back but continued down the hallway away from her. She could not be certain but thought he paused briefly and she wondered if he had indeed heard her. Beneath the large archway, throngs moved in and out of the congreget all around Maggie as she considered her friend. She looked into the large room and then back down the hall where Borador had headed. Compelled by this new curiosity she abandoned her designs to rendezvous with Dae and instead followed after Borador. Although he was no longer in her sight, she determined that he could have only one destination. Quickly she sailed forward toward the regulet.

The lone hallway joined with myriad others in the vast expanse that was the regulet. Busy spirits whisked in all directions as beams of light poured in to the central hub, yet as always there was an order and calmness to the scene. Beyond the central barrier she caught sight of Borador as he slipped behind the wall at the far end. Maggie circumnavigated the flooded pavilion in the direction Borador had disappeared. She stopped at the threshold to the veil room to determine if anyone had taken notice of her. When she was certain her present course was of no interest to the various processors who were all around her she preceded into the veil room.

A familiar sense of awe and reverence fell upon her, as it had on her first visit. The spectacular cosmos opened before her, split in two by the glorious shimmering veil. Facilitants flew back and forth from the veil to the groups of spirits waiting where the steps ended. At the top of the steps Maggie found Borador, who stood transfixed on the activity below. She drew near to him and waited quietly.

"You should not be here," Borador said without turning toward her.

"Neither should you," she replied. "And yet here we are."

Maggie drifted beside him and looked out at the beautiful shroud that parted one existence from the next. She could not help but wonder of her friend's intentions for visiting this holy place.

"Right there," Borador pointed. "Right there is the last place I saw her."

"You will see her again," Maggie assured him.

"But much will have changed," he said glumly.

"Much but not all," Maggie replied. "She will still be Vila."

"That is not what they called her," Borador said. "Her name is Atia. They do not know her and yet they named her. She does not know them and is at their mercy. How can they care for her? How can they love her when they do not know who she is?"

Maggie paused, as she was not sure how to answer or what she should say. She herself had to push the questions aside as these were not answers they would find in their current state. It would only be in through mortal sojourn and beyond that these things would be made known unto them. She searched for words of encouragement and comfort but found none. They looked on in silence as spirit after spirit was escorted to the veil by the facilitants. Something Borador had said brought a question to the surface and Maggie turned to face her friend.

"How do you know they named her Atia?" she asked.

"Dae is not the only one with friends in the regulet," Borador replied.

"So you have seen her then?"

"No," he said. "I would not recognize her anyway; she is but a seed waiting to sprout into a flower."

"You might be surprised," Maggie said. "The finites say that the eyes are a window to the soul. You may find her waiting for you in those eyes."

He turned to face her and a hint of a smile broke across his face.

"Thank you," he said.

"For what?"

"For showing kindness I do not deserve," he answered.

"You do not have to earn kindness, Borador," Maggie explained. "It has no price for it costs nothing to be kind."

"Are those more words from the finites?"

"No," Maggie said. "They are my own."

"Well then, I hope when your turn comes you will remember them," he said. "Because they are worthy of being recorded. May they one day bless our brothers and sisters."

They regarded each other warmly and their spirits glowed brightly. Maggie glanced back toward the veil and then over to the doorway through which she had entered. She remembered Dae and her desire to commune with her. She looked back at Borador who had turned his attention to the activities of the veil room.

"Will you accompany me to the congreget?" she asked.

"I would like to stay here a while longer," he said graciously.

"Very well," Maggie said. "Until our next."

With a nod Borador excused her and she moved swiftly from the room and back into the busy regulet. She took a moment to enjoy the grandeur of the immense pavilion. The walls of light that surrounded it pulsed with beams that shot in from every direction to the center of the room behind the center barrier. Maggie wondered what became of them once they reached this collection point. Did someone else know Eric as she did? The spirits moved with purpose through the regulet and she imagined that they all must be off to something interesting, but what interested her now was what Dae would have to report. She weaved through the multitude and made her way back down the hall that led to their congreget. Upon arrival she looked from side to side until she spotted her young friend. Dae appeared to be in search of something and when she saw Maggie a huge smile formed on her face. With haste they closed the gap between them until they were face-to-face.

"Salutations, Maggie," Dae said excitedly.

"Salutations, little dove," Maggie replied.

Dae's countenance grew bright and she smiled broadly. For the first time Maggie noticed a change in her friend. She was not the youthful and naïve spirit who had first entered their circle. There was a new life and confidence to her. Maggie thought that Vila would have been proud of her young protégé.

"I—" they both began in unison. Maggie stopped and Dae shrunk slightly.

"You go first," Maggie said.

"I could not find you at first," Dae said. "I was anxious to visit with you."

"Apologies," Maggie said. "I was speaking with Borador."

"Is he here?" Dae asked as she looked beyond Maggie to the spirits that filled the congreget.

"No," said Maggie. "I found him in the veil room."

"What? Why?" Dae asked with some alarm.

"All is well," Maggie assured her. "He was in search of solitude and peace."

"He misses her," Dae stated plainly.

Maggie nodded. "Did you know she is called Atia?"

"Yes, I believe it means ancient," she smiled. "It suits her, although I am not sure Vila would be pleased."

"No," Maggie grinned. "She would not."

"Should we go to him?" asked Dae.

"No," replied Maggie. "He said he would join us when he is ready."

Maggie understood her interest and concern but she wished to speak of Eric and Lindsey. When she was confident that she had given their current topic sufficient consideration, she promptly changed the subject.

"And how is your training going?" she asked.

"Very well," Dae responded. "I have learned much from Kya; she is a worthy mentor."

"And her beholden?" Maggie inquired. Dae smiled since she knew what Maggie desired.

"She is tormented," Dae answered plainly as the smile faded.

Maggie was taken aback by her answer. Tormented was a word with strong and varied implications. She feared that her torment had something to do with Eric but could not see exactly how.

"Tormented?" she finally asked.

"Yes," Dae said. "She has suffered much and carries her pain with her always. Maggie, she has been hurt so deeply by those whom she loved most, by those who ought to have cared for her and protected her."

Maggie did not know what to say. She thought of all she knew of Lindsey and what Eric thought of her. She could not fathom someone hurting her or wishing to do her harm. Dae looked at her with mournful eyes and a dimmed countenance. Although her desire was to know the cause of her pain she did not dare ask, but she waited for her friend to speak further.

"Eric is the lone bright spot in her life," Dae said. "But she is waiting for that light to leave."

"Leave?" Maggie said. "He has no desire to leave. On the contrary, his greatest desire is to be with her."

"That is good," Dae said. "I only wish she could know that and that she would trust that."

"What cause has he given her to doubt?" asked Maggie.

"Her doubt is her own," explained Dae. "The closer she lets him get, the greater her fear grows."

"What does she fear?"

"She fears the power he has to bring her low," said Dae.

"He does not wish to bring her low," Maggie said. "He wishes to know her, to love her."

"That is the power she fears."

The idea that knowledge and love could promote fear was something beyond Maggie's comprehension. For her, knowledge brought a clarity that dispelled fear. As for love, love was not something to fear, for the two stood in opposition. As He said "perfect love casteth out fear." Unable to understand Dae's revelation, Maggie shifted her focus back to Eric.

"What can he do?" she asked.

"I do not know," Dae replied. "It may be that there is nothing to be done. She will need time, that is certain, but a lifetime of reassurance may not be enough."

"I believe a lifetime is what he is hoping to give," Maggie added.

"I would be glad for that," said Dae. "If only she will let him. Maggie, inside her there is much conflict. She is torn between her feelings for him and the pain of her past."

"Is that why she does not wish to speak of home?" asked Maggie.

Dae nodded.

"Is there anything that brings her joy?"

"At times the written word offers an escape from herself," answered Dae. "Through the stories and insights of others she finds respite from her own travails. Does Eric like to read at all?"

Maggie shook her head solemnly. "He prefers a more visual medium of storytelling."

"Like Star Wars?" Dae asked.

"Yes, like Star Wars," Maggie replied.

"So you have seen it then?" she asked.

"Many times."

"Thelma knew of war," Dae said. "Vila said she was a nurse-maid to the soldiers of a great war. I cannot imagine why the stars would war with each other."

"The title is deceiving," Maggie explained. "The war takes place among the stars, not between them."

"I see," said Dae. "Does Eric enjoy war, then?"

"He has not experienced war himself," Maggie said. "But war, or at least someone's idea of war, is pervasive in much of his entertainment."

"Do you find it odd that he would find entertainment in something so violent and destructive?" asked Dae.

"There are a great many things about mortality that I find odd," answered Maggie. She was not pleased with many of her beholden's choices but did not wish to fixate on them. Dae swayed slightly to the side and looked around Maggie and her face brightened. Maggie thought she knew who she must have spotted. She turned around expecting to see Lorn and was surprised to find Borador moving slowly toward them.

"Salutations, Borador," greeted Dae.

"Salutations," was his soft and kind reply.

"We have missed you, my friend," she said.

"Apologies," he said. "I will not disappear again."

"See that you do not," Maggie interjected with a smile.

"What did I miss?" he asked.

"Well I am certain you have already learned of my assignment. Maggie and I have conspired to learn and share what a young woman thinks of her beholden," Dae replied enthusiastically.

Borador looked over at Maggie with disapproval. Maggie wanted to turn away but forced herself to meet his gaze and absorb his judgement. She was fully aware of the hazards of her actions and had made her choice. Her only trepidation was for any consequences Dae might suffer as a result.

"And how goes your conspiracy?" he asked.

"We have learned much, although we are powerless to do anything about it," Dae responded.

"That is the very reason we have been counseled not to engage in this behavior," Borador chided. "No good will come of this."

"Borador," Maggie began her defense. "We simply wished for a more complete picture. We found they both have feelings for each other. That knowledge has brought us joy. What is the harm?"

"This is their turn, their time," Borador replied. "Vila would not approve. She would tell you when you become too involved you may believe you are a part of their journey. You are not. Our job is to collect and catalog their thoughts. Find the joy in that."

Maggie felt the truth in his words. It was then that she realized she had allowed a singular desire to rob her of the joy she had. No longer did she find fulfillment in her job alone but she sought for more than she had been allotted.

"I do," Maggie responded. "You are right; of course, we ought not to have done this thing. It was foolish. Dae, forgive me for enlisting you in my folly. We cannot continue in this way."

Dae nodded and looked ashamed. At no time did Borador look upset or angered but he spoke with passion and authority. Maggie had no doubt why Vila had dubbed him her Thunderer.

"Can I ask one last thing before we fully repent?" Dae inquired.

Maggie looked to Borador. He conceded and she nodded to Dae.

"Does his uncle truly have only one tooth?"

Maggie laughed. Borador smiled but looked confused.

Fired

On the monitor the bright colors spelled Google against a white backdrop. Eric drummed his fingers gently on the top of his desk. *He'll see.* He glanced over his shoulder to the empty desk to his left. *Clear.* He swiveled slightly in his chair and looked to the closed door with the black plaque that read Bill Durbin. *All clear.* Turning back to his screen he inhaled and began to type "poetry." A list of blue underlined selections appeared below the search field. *How do I know what's good?* He checked his flanks again and typed "great poets." *William Shakespeare was a poet? Walt Whitman. Emily Dickinson. Robert Frost. William Wordsworth, that's a poet name. Maya Angelou. Edgar Allan Poe. This is impossible.* He cleared the search field and typed "poems to impress a girl." *You're better than that, Eric.*

The office door behind him opened and Eric quickly closed the window on the display. He turned around to see his lanky boss standing with his hands on his hips. *What's wrong now?* Bill ran his hand over the top of his hair and exhaled. *Isn't that gel cap rock hard?*

"Is he still not in?" Bill asked. *Nope. Thank goodness.*

"He said he had a doctor's appointment," Eric replied. *Hopefully to do something about that smell. Or maybe to remove his voice box.*

Be kind.

The white lettering appeared in front of Maggie. She filed the rest of his thoughts as it faded and disappeared.

"I know but he told me he'd be in before lunch," said Bill. *Well nobody has taken lunch yet so I guess he's still okay.*

"Have you tried calling him?" Eric asked. *Maybe he died. Now you'll feel guilty if he does.*

"Nah, it's not a big deal," said Bill. *Then why are we talking about it?* "What are you working on?" *Stink'n Mark, now he's turned his boss-attention on me.*

"Cathy is complaining that her phone is cutting out," replied Eric. "I was going to go check it out on the way to lunch." *Please don't ask me to do anything else.*

"Any idea what's causing it?" Bill asked. *Operator error? Why do you care?*

"No, I'm sure it's something stupid," Eric said. *Knowing her, it's probably nothing at all.*

The door to the hall opened and Mark sloshed in shaking a dripping wet umbrella. *Speak of the devil.* Several droplets splashed onto Eric's desk and keyboard. *Just shake that water anywhere, fella.* His head, hair and the top three quarters of his shirt were dry but his pants and shoes were soaked through. He set the umbrella next to Eric's desk and the door closed behind him.

"Speak of the devil," said Eric. *The wet devil.*

"Can you believe this weather?" Mark said. *Rain. Yeah, I can believe that it rains.*

"Everything good?" Bill asked. *Here we go.*

"Oh yeah, it was just a check-up," Mark replied. "Going in for a colonoscopy next month." *Too much information. Please don't expound. Abort. Abort.*

"Well on that note, I've got work to do," Eric said, he stood up and retrieved his phone and headphones from his desk. He shoved them in his pockets, being sure not to look up at Bill. *Flee, quickly.*

"Need any help?" Mark asked. *Oh no. I'm good.*

"Nope," said Eric. "You just sit your colon down over there and take it easy." *I'm hilarious.*

Eric stepped around the puddle beneath the dripping umbrella and pulled open the door. *Later lunes.* He looked back to see Mark sitting down at his desk and Bill returning to his office. *That could have been worse.* The door closed and he stood alone in the quiet hallway. He looked down to his right toward a group of muffled voices a few offices down before he turned and headed in the opposite direction. A turn down the first hallway he came to had him pointed straight toward the front lobby. To his right were several colorful posters of various Treat Mete dispensers. Like a vision, Lindsey passed before his eyes and disappeared around the corner. *Bright Eyes.* Eric hurried to the end of the hall and looked around the corner.

"Hey Lindsey," he called after her. *Hey'll.*

Clearly in a rush, she had already put some distance between herself and the hallway where he stood. She slowed and looked over her shoulder. *Puffy eyes. Is she crying? Stalin.* Without stopping and without a word, Lindsey continued in the direction she had been heading.

"Well hey there, Harry Haircut," called an excited voice from behind him. *Oh boy.* "You here to fix my phone?" *No, I came for the witty repartee. Just shoot me. Shoot me and take me to the hospital, I could use the time off.*

Maggie grimaced. His thoughts of late had been of a more positive nature. Many of them centered on the brighter things of his mortal journey. He had even made specific plans to improve his overall physical health and fitness. His first thoughts in the morning were of her and the opportunities that the day held and not of hardship and monotony, as they had been for so long. This still gave Maggie great hope; although she now saw how easily he fell back into old habits and patterns of thought.

I hope she's okay. He turned around to look down at the frumpy woman with curly hair who sat behind the semi-circle desk in the front lobby with a forced disingenuous smile. *Make this quick and go check on Lindsey.*

"Let's have a look," Eric replied as he slid around behind the desk. Cathy got up from her chair and stood against the wall behind her desk. *Whoah, that perfume is kick'n. My nostils. What is that? Plum?* Eric sat down in her chair and lifted the receiver on the phone. He held it to his ear and the dull sound of dial tone filled

Maggie's box. He pressed several numbers and a variety of beeps sounded before a soft ringing began. *Gloomy.* While he waited, he peered out at the sheets of rain pouring beyond the large glass wall at the front of the lobby. *Gray sky's gonna clear up.*

"This is Bill," answered a voice through the phone. *Could she be mad at me?*

"Hey Bill, it's Eric," he answered. "Just testing the phone. Can you hear me okay?" *Did I do something, or say something? Who hurt her? I bet it was Little Stalin. Forget the phone. Go check on Lindsey.*

"Yeppers," said Bill. "Loud and clear." *Yeppers? Sheesh.*

"There's no cutting out?" asked Eric. *I knew it.*

"Nope," replied Bill. *Of course not.*

"Well it doesn't do it all the time, Franky Fix-It," Cathy said defensively. *One more nickname and I'm walking.*

"Thanks, Bill," he said before hanging up the handset. *Don't yell at her. Be kind.*

Maggie was happy that these thoughts were his own. His nature was to be kind, but he often gave in to the frustrations he felt so deeply from his interactions with others. *I should have followed her, made sure she is okay. This is a waste of time.*

"Sometimes it cuts out when I'm using email at the same time," she suggested. *There is no connection. Please stop talking.* "And it happens more in the afternoon than in the morning. Maybe the phone gets tired. I know I do." *Ha ha. Hilarious.*

"Maybe it needs a nap," he said dryly. *Don't encourage her.*

"Hee hee," she giggled. "You're so funny." *I know.* She reached out and slapped him on the back. *No touching. Headphones.* He reached down and touched his pocket to feel the coiled up cords of his headphones. He picked up Cathy's phone and held it upside down to look underneath it. With one hand he followed the cord until it disappeared through a hole in the desktop. He bent down and looked under the desk. *Holy rat's nest, Batman.* There was a mess of tangled cables and wires that ran along the floor.

"Could it be something I'm doing?" she asked earnestly. *Probably.*

He reached into his pocket and pulled out his cell and headphones. "This might take a while. If you want to take a break, this is probably a good time." *Just go.* He slid off the seat and fixed his headphones in each ear. *Please go.*

"Sounds good to me," she replied. "I need to visit the little girl's room." *I did not need to know that, ever. Geez. Just leave.*

Eric got down on his hands and knees beneath the desk. Cathy's feet disappeared from behind the chair and Eric turned his attention to his phone. With a quick flick with his thumb he selected shuffle and horns began to play throughout Maggie's box. *Pack it up, pack it in, let me begin. I came to win, battle me that's a sin.* Eric pulled on the tangled mess of wires and the knot tightened. *Perfect, just perfect.* He blew at a dust bunny that brushed across his nose. *Get up, stand up c'mon throw your hands up. If you've got the feeling, jump across the ceiling.* He let out an audible growl as he struggled to free a single cable from the interwoven spool. *How does this even happen?*

Feelin, funkin, amps in the trunk and I got more rhymes than there's cops at a Dunkin' Donuts shop, sho' nuff, I got props. A pair of feet appeared from behind the desk.

Look up.

Back already? Give me a break.

Look up.

Eric turned toward the feet and hit his head on a sharp mounting bracket beneath the desk. *Ouch! Come on, Cathy!*

"Can you just back off for a minute!" he barked. *Go away. Ow!*

He looked up to see a slender pair of legs disappear around the corner of the desk. *Not Cathy. Shoot. Come on Eric. Ow, am I bleeding?* He felt the top of his head. *No blood. Man that hurt.* The secure lock clicked and the heavy lobby door opened. The noise of rainfall from outside flooded into the room for a moment before the door clicked shut again. *I came to get down, I came to get down, so get out your seat and jump around!* Eric scooted out from under the desk. He craned his neck to peer over top of the desk and look toward the front of the lobby. Beyond the glass wall he saw a slender blonde woman in khaki slacks and a red sweater walking toward the parking lot in the pouring rain. *Lindsey. Bright Eyes.*

She needs you.

Way to go, idiot.

Get up.

Dae burst into the box. With a start Maggie turned her attention from her beholden to face her friend's unexpected entrance.

"Oh Maggie!" Dae exclaimed. "She is going to take her life."

"What?" Maggie asked. "Slow down."

"Lindsey," she explained. "She has chosen to end her life."

"No," Maggie looked back to the portal.

Get up.

Eric sat back and rested his head against a tall filing cabinet. *Jump around, jump around, jump around.*

"Maggie, what do we do?"

She looked back to Dae, who wore a horrified expression. *Jump up, jump up and get down.*

Get up.

Back through the portal Eric still sat on the ground and rubbed the back of his head.

"Get up, Eric," Maggie whispered. She walked around the oval platform and slowly drew near the portal.

Get up.

"Come on, Eric. Get up."

Eric lifted his head to see over the desk. *Where did she go?* The gray sky hovered low over the cars in the parking lot. He let his body relax and fell gently back against the filing cabinet. *Jump, jump, jump, jump, jump, jump, jump.*

"She is going to kill herself," Dae said again from the far corner of the box. "She believes no one will care, and she wonders if anyone will even notice. Oh Maggie, I cannot bear the thought."

Maggie was so close to the portal now she could feel the energy pulse through her. *Jump, jump, jump, jump.* "She needs you, Eric."

He closed his eyes. *You screwed up again. Where is she going? Maybe you could take her an umbrella and apologize. Tell her you didn't know it was her. No, she probably needs some time. Call her tonight.*

"Maggie, she will not be there tonight," Dae said. "The last thought I saw she was going to the river. She is heading there now!" *Jump, jump.*

"I am her only hope," Maggie said. *Jump, jump.*

"What?" Dae asked. "What do you mean?"

Maggie thought of all the promptings Eric had received and all he had ignored. Never before had a prompting been so significant or the consequences so dire. In an instant Maggie considered the ramifications for Lindsey and Eric if this prompting went unheeded. Not only would Lindsey's progression be irreparably cut short, but she also feared Eric would not recover.

"She needs him and he needs me," Maggie said. *Jump, jump.*

"Maggie, no."

"Until our next, my sweet dove."

She looked back at her friend and pressed against the portal. She felt a pressure she had never felt before. It pushed upon her from all sides. There was an intense pull that drew her out of the box. A bright white light consumed her field of vision as she was rapidly pulled away from her station. Dae grew smaller and smaller as did the oval platform between she and Maggie.

"Maggie!" Dae's voice echoed into the void and sounded distant and hollow.

The light quickly faded to darkness and closed in until all was black.

The Leap

Maggie felt a dull throbbing back and behind her. There was a sensation of stinging and sweetness she had never felt before. She felt confined and could not move. Directly in front of her she saw a pair of legs, bent at the knees. The right leg moved slightly and a small gray clump of dust and lint wafted gently into the air and settled back onto the floor. *Word to your moms, I came to drop bombs, I got more rhymes than the Bible's got Psalms, and just like the Prodigal Son I've returned.*

"Eric," she said. "Get up. Get up!"

He quickly removed his headphones and scanned the empty room from side to side. *Nobody. What was that? I swore I heard someone.*

"Hello?"

"Get up," she repeated. "Go after her." *Who's that?*

Eric drew his legs in and rolled up onto his knees. *What's going on?* He reached up and put his hand on the desk. As he did Maggie felt a coolness at the end of his appendage.

I felt that, she thought. *It is cold.*

"Hello?" Eric called again. "Is somebody there?" *Am I being punked?*

"Eric, Lindsey needs you," Maggie said. "You have to go after her, now!"

There was a pounding sound that echoed all around her. It grew louder and more rapid. Eric looked under the desk and from one end of the room to the other. *I'm losing it.*

"You are not losing it," Maggie said. *Whoa! What? Mind reader.*

"Who are you?" *You're going crazy.*

"You are not going crazy," Maggie assured him. "Please, there is no time. You must hurry." *I'm definitely crazy. Must have hit my head harder than I thought. Does my insurance cover a shrink?*

"Listen," Maggie said. "I am your conscience. I need you to find Lindsey right now. It is very important." *My conscious? Jiminy Cricket.*

"Now!"

All right! He came to his feet and walked around the desk. *Should I get an umbrella?*

"Just go!" Maggie shouted.

Fine!

Eric hurried to the front door and pushed it open. *My conscience is awfully bossy all of a sudden.* A wall of rain fell from the building's eave and pounded the pavement in front of him. Maggie felt the cool air rush against Eric's skin. He took in a deep breath.

That feels amazing, she thought.

He scanned from one end of the parking lot to the other and saw only dormant cars beneath the gray clouds. *She's gone.* From his periphery Maggie spotted a flash of red appear briefly between the trees lining the street in the distance.

"There," she said. "To your left."

Where?

"I don't see anything," Eric replied. *Where to my left? What am I looking for?*

"A red sweater," Maggie said. "She is wearing a red sweater."

Yeah, red sweater.

Still under the protection of the building eave overhead, Eric leaned to his left and strained his neck to peer up the road. *Red. There she is.* He stepped out into the rain and jogged up the sidewalk that ran across the front of the building. When he reached the end he could see straight down to the end of the lane. A blonde-haired woman in a red sweater was approaching the corner of 28th and K Street. *Hurry.*

Yes, hurry, Maggie thought.

He raced down the sidewalk and nearly tripped on a raised concrete slab. *Flip! Stupid sidewalk.* Maggie felt a sting from beneath her and a tiny throbbing sensation.

Is that his toe? she wondered.

He raced past the grand old oak trees that separated the Treat Mete parking lot from the public walkway.

What does tree bark feel like? Maggie wondered.

Just ahead, the blonde woman in the red sweater stopped at the intersection. *Call to her.*

"Lindsey!" Eric shouted. *That sounded panicked. Calm down, you'll scare her.*

Lindsey turned around with a startled expression on her face. *Bright Eyes.* Maggie could feel a swelling rise up in Eric's chest. He strode to a stop a few feet from her. They looked at one another in silence for several seconds while Eric breathed deeply and tried to catch his breath. *You gotta get in better shape.* Lindsey wiped her face with the sleeves of her sweater. *Crying. Is that the rain or are those tears? No, she's definitely crying.*

"Where are you going?" he asked. *Too forward?*

"I . . ." she choked up as she glanced over her shoulder. *Go on. It's okay. I'm here.*

She looked down at the pavement beneath her feet. Her body tightened and contorted slightly. *What's wrong? Say something.*

"Are you okay?" asked Eric. *Of course she's not.*

Tears welled up in her eyes as she looked up to meet Eric's gaze. She pressed her lips together and shook her head. *What can I do? What should I say?*

"Tell her she is beautiful," Maggie suggested.

"No!" Eric shouted aloud.

"What?" Lindsey asked. *Ugh.*

"Um, I mean, no, I know you're not okay," he replied. *This is not going well.*

Her lower lip began to quiver as the steady rain dripped down on them. A lone car slowly pulled through the intersection behind her and highlighted the solitude they enjoyed. The streets were empty and it seemed as if the homes on the opposite side of the street were all sleeping.

"I can hear your thoughts," Maggie explained. "You don't have to speak."

Well what do I do now?

"You can start by getting her out of this rain," said Maggie. *Right, good idea.*

"Let's go inside and we can talk about it," said Eric.

"I can't," Lindsey shook her head and her voice cracked. "I got fired." *Stalin! What a jerk!*

"I'm sorry, I . . ." he began. *Now what?* He shifted awkwardly from side to side and looked to the street beyond her.

"You cannot let her go," Maggie said. "She needs you, Eric."

I know. Think, Eric, think.

"My place is just up the road and around the corner," he said. "I've got towels and an electric blanket." *Electric blanket? Did that sound weird?*

"No, thanks," said Lindsey. "I'm . . . I'm just gonna go."

"Do not let her leave, Eric," said Maggie.

What do you want me to do, kidnap her?

"Try again," she replied. "Try something else."

All right, something else.

"Are you sure?" he asked. "I've got hot chocolate."

He tilted his head, flashed a big grin, and raised his eyebrows hopefully. *You sound like you are trying to lure her back to your house. Creeper territory. Reel it in, Eric.* She did not answer but glanced back over her shoulder and fidgeted nervously.

"Look, I don't want you to leave," he said. "If you'll let me, I'd like to help you." *I think you're great. I think I may love you. Please don't go.*

"Tell her that," Maggie said.

No! Not a chance. Are you crazy? Wait, am I crazy?

"Have courage, Eric," urged Maggie. "Love recognizes no barriers. With love there is always hope."

Well then I hope she can't hear you, because then she'll definitely think I'm a nut job.

"It's just a couple of blocks that way," he said and pointed up the road behind her. "You were heading that direction anyway. What do you say?" *Please say yes.*

She nodded. "Okay." *Sweet! Hallelujah!*

Eric smiled and walked to stand beside her. They each checked to see that the way was clear and then made their way across the street. The rain continued to drizzle down as they walked up the empty street.

What does it feel like to embrace? thought Maggie.

"Put your arm around her," she said.

You better quit it with that craziness. I mean it.

They turned the corner and walked up a pair of steps to his front door. *Did I leave the light on?* A soft glow emanated from his front window and contrasted with the mute gray gloom outside. Eric reached into his pocket. *Nuts. My keys are on my desk back at the office.* He grinned sheepishly at Lindsey and kicked over a faux rock beside the entryway. Beneath the plastic rock was nothing but dry dirt. *What? Where's the spare key?* Eric walked up to the front door and turned the handle. *Unlocked.* He gently pushed open the door. Light and music poured out through the doorway. Music blared from his entertainment center and Eric heard the tune of "I'm bringing sexy back." A large bearded man in a black t-shirt bounced back and forth in the kitchen behind the counter and sang along with the music. *Dave.* Eric stepped through the doorway and pressed the button at the base of his entertainment center. The music stopped and the man in the kitchen spun around.

"Dave," Eric said. *Not now.*

"Hey man," Dave said. "What are you doing here?" *I live here, jerky.*

"Dude, what's going on?" asked Eric.

"Just making some hot cocoa, brother," Dave replied. *Of course you are. This is my life. Terrible timing.*

"Oh wonderful, I like Dave," Maggie said.

That's enough out of you.

"Who's your friend?" Dave asked with a nod toward Lindsey.

"This is Lindsey," replied Eric. "Come on in." He motioned to her. "Lindsey, this is Dave." *A homeless lunatic who is making hot chocolate in my kitchen while listening to Justin Timberlake.*

Lindsey stepped into the front room with her arms folded tight across her body. *She's wet and cold. Go get her a towel.*

"Well hey there, darl'n," Dave said. "Can I interest you in a hot cup of cocoa?"

"That's very kind," Lindsey said. "Thank you."

Freaking Dave. I was supposed to be the kind one.

"Have a seat," Eric said. "I'll go get you a towel."

Lindsey sat down on the futon as Eric made his way to the hall closet. As he passed the kitchen Dave was carefully carrying a mug toward the living room. With a wink and a nod toward Lindsey he smiled at Eric. "She's cute," he whispered and gave him a thumbs-up.

Oh boy, this is not going like I imagined.

Eric shook his head and hurried to the small closet outside the bathroom. *Towel.* He pulled open the door and removed a navy blue cotton towel from the top shelf. After a quick smell check he headed back toward the living room. He heard Lindsey giggle. *Her laugh.* Maggie felt a swelling pressure again in his chest. *His heart. Love,* she thought.

In the living room he found Dave comfortably lounging on one side of the futon opposite a wet and cold Lindsey holding a steaming mug with the Star Wars logo on it. *My favorite mug.*

"Here you go," Eric extended the towel toward her. *Be warm.*

"Thank you," she placed the mug on the armrest and rapped the towel around her shoulders.

"I can go get that electric blanket if you like."

"No thank you," she replied. "This is fine." *Stop pushing the electric blanket.*

Eric looked back and forth between Dave and Lindsey. *Where do I sit? Squeeze in between them? Too awkward. Grab a seat.* He spun around and pulled a brown ottoman to the center of the room and sat down facing the futon. *No Dave, let me sit on the ottoman. It's fine, really.* Lindsey took a sip of her hot chocolate and held the cup in her hands.

"So you're Eric's brother?" she asked. *Brother? No.*

"Nah," Dave answered. "We're just good buddies." *Don't say buddies.*

A cold shiver shot up Eric's spine and he shook slightly. *Cold, we're cold,* Maggie thought. Eric folded his arms and touched his wet shirtsleeves. *Wet. Water is cold.*

"Let me get you a cup of cocoa, brother," Dave said as he jumped to his feet. *About time.*

"Thanks," said Eric. *That's why she thinks we're brothers, because of Hulk Hogan over there.*

"So he's your roommate," Lindsey asked Eric. *No. Not even close.*

"No," replied Eric. "Dave, well . . . he lives where he likes, mostly in the park." *Bum.*

The cupboards banged shut and a cup clinked and clanked against a pot. *I want to feel what glass feels like,* thought Maggie. Lindsey and Eric looked into the kitchen. Lindsey leaned toward Eric. *Bright Eyes. She's so pretty.*

"He's homeless?" she whispered. *Basically.*

Dave returned with two cups of steaming hot chocolate. He handed one to Eric and took his seat on the futon next to Lindsey. *Bless you.* Maggie felt a sensation in Eric's extremities that grew stronger and gradually flowed down his arms. *Warmth,* she thought. Eric raised the cup to his lips and sipped the brown liquid inside. The heat radiated down his throat and Maggie felt it fill his insides.

Tingling swept through his body until millions of tiny explosions ignited in his brain.

"Oh," Maggie exclaimed. "Oh, that is wonderful." *You're still here? Shoot! Crazy town.*

"Perfect, just perfect," Eric muttered.

"What's that?" Dave asked. *Uh. Think fast. Homeless.*

"Lindsey asked if you were homeless," Eric replied. *He'll love that.*

"If a man goes to deepest darkest Africa on safari," Dave began. *Here we go.* "And he sleeps in a tent or in a tree or just right on the ground, he's called an explorer. I choose to do the very same thing in the heart of the city and I'm called homeless. It's semantics really." *There it is.*

"It's not semantics, it's called society," Eric rebutted. "This isn't deepest darkest Africa, it's Sacramento. It's just the way things are. You can choose the Congo or a condo." *Hobo.*

"Bah," Dave said. "You've been brainwashed. That's what they want you to think."

"Who's they?" asked Lindsey. *Here it comes. Conspiracy.*

"Home manufactures, lenders, bankers, government, they're all in on it," replied Dave. *Wee.* "Think about it, who benefits from you confining yourself to four walls and a ceiling?" *Lunatic.*

"You!" shouted Eric. "You do, ya psycho. You benefit. There's shelter, protection, security, comfort. Those are benefits, enjoyed by people who 'confine' themselves to it."

"Ah, you're a lemming," rebutted Dave. "You'll follow the crowd even if it's right over a cliff." *What cliff?*

"Okay Mr. Intentionally Homeless," Eric said. "If you don't need shelter then why are you here? Could it be the rain pouring down on your life's safari?" *Boom. Mic drop.*

"Fine," Dave came to his feet. "You make a guy some hot chocolate—"

"It's my hot chocolate," interrupted Eric. *And my Star Wars mug.*

"And this is the thanks you get," continued Dave. "I'll go. I don't need all this. I love the rain." *Go then. See ya later Gene Kelly. Have a ball.*

Dave placed his mug on the counter and walked to the front door. *Where are you going? You're not going anywhere.* He placed his hand on the doorknob and turned back to the room. *Go on, Rain Gosling.* "It was a pleasure meeting you Miss Lindsey. Good day to you." *I'm not buying it.*

He gestured back at Eric with a flick of his head and pulled open the door. The rain fell in buckets beyond the threshold. There were several inches of standing water on the walkway and the island of grass beside it was complete submerged.

"Oh dear," said Maggie. *He's not going anywhere.*

"Do you want an umbrella?" asked Eric. *Go on, I dare you.*

"No," replied Dave. "I wouldn't want to trouble you. I'll be fine." *Okay, that's enough.*

Dave hesitated at the door as he, Lindsey, and Eric stared out at the downpour.

"Would you come back in here, you crazy hobo," Eric said. *Or don't. I don't care.*

"Yes, please," Lindsey begged. "You can't go out in that." *He's an explorer; he'll be fine.*

"Eric, be kind," Maggie chided. *I was only joking. It's called sarcasm.*

"Well, all right," Dave closed the door. "But only for Lindsey's sake."

Dave winked at her. *Easy fella.* Lindsey smiled and sipped her hot chocolate. *What now?* Dave sat back on the futon and the trio silently drank from their cups and listened to the rainfall outside. Eric fixed his gaze directly on Lindsey. There was a far off look in her eyes. *What is she thinking about?*

Ask her, thought Maggie.

"Do you want to hear the story of how I saved our boy Eric here from a pack of wild dogs?" asked Dave. *A pack?*

"It was two dogs and I didn't need to be saved," interjected Eric. *It is a good story though.*

"So they were bearing down on him just outside the Arby's on J Street," Dave went on. "Teeth showing, snarling, growling, and foaming at the mouth. He was backed up to the dumpster between the wall and the building with nowhere to turn." *Master exaggerator.*

"When out of nowhere this bum jumps out of the dumpster, grabs the bag from my hand and starts unwrapping MY sandwiches and throwing them at the dogs," Eric added. *Five for $5.*

"Then I yell, 'Run for it' and we jumped over the dogs and hauled butt outta there," Dave finished with a big grin. *Heck of a first meeting.*

"And I haven't been able to get rid of him ever since," joked Eric. *And I wouldn't want to.*

"Nope," Dave chuckled. "Somebody's got to look out for ya."

Lindsey smiled brightly. *Love that smile.*

Did we do it? Maggie wondered. *Will she be okay now?*

"So you two met at work?" Dave asked Lindsey. *Oh no.*

The smile on Lindsey's face faded. *Crud. Jump in. Change the subject. Save her.*

"Come to think of it, why aren't you at work now? You playing hooky?" Dave teased with a raise of the eyebrow. *Stop.*

"Actually I was fired today," Lindsey looked down at the ground. *Way to go, Dave!*

The room fell silent; it was as if all the air was sucked out through a vacuum. Eric shot Dave a dirty look. Dave cringed and hunched his shoulders with a look of contrition.

This too shall pass, Maggie thought.

Change the subject.

"Well that's a real downer," said Dave. "With the rain too, you're having yourself a day, aren't ya?" *Are you trying to make it worse? Stop.*

"Tell her this will pass," Maggie said.

"No," Eric whispered aloud. Dave and Lindsey both looked over at him. *Shoot. Would you please be quiet? I'm a crazy person, I'm a crazy person, I'm a crazy person. Save this.*

"I mean, uh, no," he began. "It's not a downer. It's their loss. You don't need that place." *Nice save.*

"I need a job to live," replied Lindsey. *Good point. Terrible save. Strike one.*

"Nah," said Dave with a dismissive wave of his hand. "I haven't had a job in years and I get by." *Stop talking Dave.*

"What he means to say is this isn't the end of the world," Eric interrupted with a stern look in his friend's direction. "You'll find something else. Look at it this way; it's a chance for a new start." *That sounds pretty good.*

"This was my new start," she choked up and her voice cracked. *Oh no. Please don't cry.*

"Well that's the beautiful thing about life, darl'n," Dave said with a grin. "There's no limit on new starts." *Where did that come from?*

"That is beautiful," said Maggie.

It kind of is. Wait, am I agreeing with myself?

"He's right," said Eric. *Heads Up.* "And on that note let's start anew right now. You ever play Heads Up?" *This will definitely lighten the mood. Let's do this. Game time.*

"I don't think so," she replied. *No problem.*

"Oh, I love this game," Maggie said.

You're not playing Ms. Voice-In-My-Head.

"It's like charades," Eric explained. "It's fun. Dave and I will show you."

Eric pulled out his phone and scrolled through his apps with the screen in front of him. *Is his phone made of glass?* Maggie wondered. Dave sat on the edge of the futon with a big smile on his face. Eric shifted on the ottoman to face him. *Category?*

"What category do you want?" asked Eric. *Friends? Football? Movies?*

"Do the celebrity one," Dave replied. *Sweet.*

"All right," Eric pressed an icon on his phone and held it to his forehead facing Dave. "You ready?"

"I was born ready," replied Dave. *Oh brother.*

Eric glanced over at Lindsey and smiled. *Is she into this? Is she okay? Bright Eyes.* Maggie heard a steady beeping tone coming from the phone. Dave shifted and moved closer to Eric until he was barely touching the padding beneath him. There was one long tone and Dave waved his arms frantically.

"Oh, WOLVERINE!" he shouted.

"Hugh Jackman," Eric answered. *Boom.*

He flipped the phone backwards and Maggie felt the tiny hair follicles on his head, as they were momentarily disturbed by the movement.

What an odd sensation, she thought.

"She's hot!" Dave yelled. *Not helpful.* "Um, blondish red hair." *Still not helpful.* "Uh, married Tom Cruise."

"Nicole Kidman," answered Eric. *Nailed it.*

"Yep," Dave confirmed as Eric flipped the phone once more against his head. "Oh, he was in *Alias.*" *JJ Abrams. Monster-in-law.*

"The guy from *Never Been Kissed*?" asked Eric. *Michael something.*

"No, uh, *The Hangover,*" Dave waved his arms as if beckoning Eric to continue. *Was Zach Galifianakis in Alias?* "A-team." *What? Uh, um. Ah!* "Rocket Raccoon."

"Bradley Cooper," Eric said jumping off the ottoman.

"Got it," said Dave. *Bradley Cooper was in* Alias*? Oh yeah.* Eric flipped the phone back.

"Pass," Dave waved his arm sideways. Eric flipped the phone forward and glimpsed at a red screen with white letters that read Michael Cera. *Arrested Development. Zombieland. Come on, Dave. That's an easy one.* "Oh, late night talk show host." *Letterman.*

"Dave Letterman?" Eric interrupted. *Leno. Carson.*

"Younger, black hair," Dave beckoned him to continue with wide eyes. *Fallon. Kimmel.*

"Jimmy Fallon?"

Dave shook his head. "Cable."

"Stephen Colbert," Maggie said excitedly.

Not now.

"Stephen Colbert?" Eric said aloud.

"Yes," Dave said as a buzzing noise sounded from Eric's phone. *Nailed it.*

"I got it," Maggie giggled. "Oh, I think he is very clever."

I didn't need your help. I would have gotten that on my own. Or did get it on my own? Did I?

"Eventually," said Maggie.

Watch yourself. I'm not afraid of a lobotomy. Yes I am.

"Four out of five, not bad," Dave said. "Your turn, darl'n." *Don't call her that.*

Lindsey was tucked back comfortably in the corner of the futon. She sat up as Dave and Eric turned to her. The pleased look on her face melted to a grimace. *Maybe this was a bad idea.*

"I don't really know celebrities," she said. *No worries.*

"That's okay," Eric assure her. "There are other categories. Or we can set it to random. It's just for fun. You don't have to be crazy like old Dave." *Psycho hobo.*

"Crazy?" Dave said. "I'm the master of this game." *Alias?*

"You said *Alias* for Bradley Cooper," rebutted Eric. *Limitless, Silver Linings Playbook.*

"He was in *Alias*," replied Dave. *He's a movie star! Start with that.*

"Eric, does this really matter?" Maggie asked. "After all, this is for fun. For Lindsey."

Fine.

"Fine, you're right," Eric conceded. He handed the phone to Lindsey. "Here you pick."

She put down her mug and took the phone from Eric. Her fingers brushed against his. Eric's heart rate increased and Maggie felt a warmth in his face. *Again, please.*

He loves her, Maggie thought.

Lindsey fiddled with the phone with a puzzled look on her face. She finally tapped the screen and looked up at Eric. *Bright Eyes.*

"Okay," she said. "Ready?" *Born ready. Don't say that.*

"Yep."

She placed his phone on her forehead and the beeps coincided with a numerical count down. Following a long beep the screen displayed in white letters the word *triangle. Three sides.*

"It has three sides," Eric started. "Shape."

"Triangle," Lindsey said as she hopped up and down slightly and flipped the phone.

"Good clues," Maggie said.

Not now.

Fiction. "Oh, you like this," Eric pointed both arms straight at her.

"Books," she replied with a loud yelp. *Close. Keep going.*

"Genre," he motioned for her to keep guessing.

"Mystery, romance, adventure?" *No.*

"Not little, major, broader." *You got this.*

"Fiction!" she yelled. *Yes!*

"Bingo."

She flipped the phone and the two words appeared. *Koala bear.*

"Uh, Australia, furry, cuddly, cute," Eric shouted.

"Koala bear." *Yes!*

"Yeah!" *She is great. I love her. Focus.* Another upward flip of the phone revealed the word Madonna. *Easy.*

"Like a virgin!" Eric shouted.

Lindsey recoiled and contorted her face. *Uh oh. Save this.* "Um, Vogue," Eric rotated his hands over and around his face in a box frame motion. Lindsey's face relaxed and a faint smile began to show.

"Madonna?" Lindsey asked. *Thank goodness.*

"Yes," Eric replied with a sigh of relief. *Next.* The white words *peanut butter* appeared on the screen following another flip. *Allergic.*

"Ooh, you're allergic to it," Eric shot both hands toward Lindsey. *Too aggressive?*

"Peanuts," she excitedly replied. *No.* Eric jumped up from the ottoman and frantically motioned with his hands for her to continue. *Keep going.*

"Peanut butter," she jumped up and shouted as the phone made a buzzing noise. *YES!*

Eric smiled and stepped toward Lindsey with both hands over his head. She raised her hands but missed Eric's hands and grazed his chin with her fingers while his palm struck her gently on the forehead. He made a half-hearted attempt to hug her before they both placed their hands at their sides and looked down at the beige carpet. *Awkward. So awkward. Kill me.*

"Do not say that Eric," Maggie chided. "Not even joking."

Please go away, Crazy Voice.

"Wow," Dave called from the futon. "You two make quite a couple." *We really do.*

"We're not a couple," said Lindsey. *Ouch. She doesn't like me. I'm a fool.*

"She does like you, Eric," Maggie said.

I'm arguing with myself. Why is this happening to me?

"You are not arguing with yourself. I am not in your head. Well, I am in your head, but I am not you."

I don't even know what that means. Am I schizophrenic? Would a schizophrenic even ask that? Maybe.

I used to think he was so smart, thought Maggie.

"Oh, I thought you two were dating," said Dave. *Almost.*

"We're going out tomorrow," Eric looked over at Lindsey for reassurance. *Right?*

Lindsey looked anxiously out the window. *What was that? Is that a no?* Eric followed her gaze and saw just a few random drops fall from the eave over the window. The sky was a much darker gray as the daylight had begun to fade. *She's going to leave. Say something.*

"The rain stopped," she observed. *You don't have to go.* "I should be going." *Don't go.*

"Don't let her go," Maggie ordered. *Are we back to kidnapping again? We. I am schizo.*

"Stay," Eric pleaded. "You don't have to go." *I want you to stay.*

"Tell her that," Maggie urged.

No.

"Thank you, but I've got some things I need to sort out," she handed Eric his cell phone and the fluffy blue towel. "This was fun. I really needed it, more than you know." *Me too.*

"Of course," said Eric. "Can I walk you home?" *Say yes.*

"No, thank you," she said. "I need to think." *I can think. I'm a good thinker.*

She walked over to the door and turned the doorknob. Dave stood up and walked next to Eric. Lindsey pulled open the door and turned to face them.

"I can be real quiet," said Eric. "You won't even know I'm there." *That sounded creepy.*

Lindsey laughed. *That laugh. That smile. Bright Eyes.* "I'm fine. Really, I am. Thank you."

"I'll see you tomorrow night then," Eric said. *Say yes, say yes, say yes.*

"Yeah," she smiled. "Tomorrow night." *Yay!*

"I can't wait." *Easy cowboy. Don't be too eager.*

"Me too."

Maybe she is going to be all right, Maggie hoped.

She stepped over the threshold and started up the walkway. Eric shadowed her out onto the doorstep. The branches of the tree-lined street swayed gently in the breeze and a few leaves floated to the ground.

Cold, this is definitely cold, thought Maggie. *It feels amazing. I think I like the cold.*

Dave stepped onto the doorstep next to Eric as Lindsey turned and headed up the sidewalk. She turned back with a sheepish wave and smiled. Eric and Dave waved back. *So cute. Is it tomorrow yet?*

"I like that girl," said Dave. "You better lock that up." *What? What does that mean?*

"What are you talking about?" asked Eric.

"You know, put a ring on it," Dave pointed to his ring finger. *Let's get through a date first.*

"Idiot," Eric smiled and shook his head. Lindsey disappeared beyond their field of view.

"I think we did it," Maggie said.

Did what?

"She is going to be okay."

Okay, you can go then. Bye bye.

What Now?

Thin lines of daylight bled through the blinds and striped the beige carpet. *Get up. Time to make the donuts.* Eric swung his feet off the bed and onto the floor. *Ugh. Work.* He rubbed his eyes and yawned. *The voice. Is it gone?*

"Are you still here?" *Please say no. Actually don't say anything.*

"Yes I am here," Maggie replied. *Crap on a cracker. This isn't happening.*

"What do you want from me?" Eric buried his head in his hands and rubbed his face vigorously. *I've completely lost it.*

"I came to help you, to help Lindsey," Maggie explained. *I do not know what to do now,* she thought.

"Came?" asked Eric. "Came from where?"

"The Department of Thoughts and Records," Maggie replied.

That sounds made up.

"I am your curator."

My what? Is this for real?

"Eric, this is real," Maggie said. "I am real."

Who are you?

"I am called Maggie."

"Maggie?" asked Eric. *Female.* "You're a girl."

"I am a daughter, yes."

That explains the soft voice. Whose daughter?

"How are you speaking to me and how can you hear what I'm thinking?" *Can you hear what I'm thinking? Pink dragons.*

"Each curator has a connection with their beholden," explained Maggie. "I can hear all of your thoughts. That connection allowed me to come here. And pink dragons are imaginary."

She's good. Or I'm good? Or crazy. Crazy good? Eric tried to swallow and Maggie felt an uncomfortable tug in his throat. His lips were dry and there was a dull pain where a crack had formed.

He is thirsty, I am nearly certain thought Maggie. *I do hope he seeks relief soon.*

He stood up from his bed and massaged his toes with the carpet threads.

That is pleasant, she thought. Following another yawn, he stretched his arms wide before exiting the bedroom through the open door. He marched down the hall and straight into the kitchen. When his bare feet landed on the linoleum floor a stinging sensation tingled his soles.

Oh that is magnificent, Maggie thought. *I like the cold.*

"So you came from the department of thoughts and things, where is that?" *Albuquerque?*

He opened the cupboard and pulled out a glass with a purple and grey crown on it and the white letters SK. *Kings. Arco.*

"It is perched on the star nearest the Vigilux nebula," Maggie stated.

The what nebula? Unimportant. Why is she here?

"You said you came to help," said Eric. "Help with what?" *Dating?*

"Lindsey needed you, Eric," said Maggie. "But you were not listening."

Listening to what?

Eric stuck the glass under the faucet and turned the nozzle on the right. Clear water poured into the glass.

Beautiful, Maggie thought. He turned the nozzle back to the left and raised the full glass to his lips. Cold water sailed down his throat.

Ooh, that is wonderful. Maggie thought.

Can I drown her out with this water?

"You were not listening to your prompting," explained Maggie.

Guess not.

"What prompting?"

"To look up, to get up, that she needed you," said Maggie. *I'm confused.*

"So you came here to yell those things at me?"

"That is correct," she said.

Why now?

"It was urgent, the moment of her greatest need."

Fired. Alone. Sad.

Eric put down his glass and pulled a green twist tie from a clear plastic bag. He removed two slices of bread and popped them in the silver toaster to the right of the oven.

Oh toast, she thought. *I have always wanted to try that.*

The red elements inside the toaster began to glow and Maggie felt the warmth from it on Eric's cheeks.

That is also pleasant, she thought. *Warmth.*

"So why are you still here?" he asked. *Mission accomplished. You can go.* "In the movies when your guardian angel shows up, it's usually until they get their wings and stuff and then they leave. Do you need a letter of recommendation or something? I'm happy to write one."

"I am not a guardian angel, that is a different department," said Maggie. "And I am afraid it is not that simple. I do not know how to leave."

Uh oh.

"You can't go back the way you came?" *Just turn around and scoot on back to the Whoobadoo nebula.*

"Our connection is how I am able to be here," she explained. "It is not something I know how to break or reverse, nor am I permitted to."

Wait, what?

"Are you saying you're trapped here in my head?" *Forever?*

"For now."

Great, just great. I'm not crazy, I'm possessed. Much better.

"You remember I can hear you?" Maggie asked.

Don't think of anything. Toast. That's something, genius.

Two golden brown pieces of bread jumped up out of the toaster. *Toast toast toast toast.* Eric opened the cupboard next to the fridge and pulled out a small white plate. He inhaled and as the warm air passed through his nostrils Maggie experienced a new and pleasant aroma.

What is that? thought Maggie. He reached in the drawer beneath the cupboard and retrieved a silver butter knife.

"Oh that is delightful," said Maggie.

What is?

"What are you talking about?" asked Eric.

"I think it is the bread?" asked Maggie. "That is wonderful."

It's toast.

"Have you never smelled toast before?" asked Eric. *That's not possible.*

"I have never smelled anything before, except the dust from under the desk, the rain, Lindsey's perfume, hot cocoa, wet Dave . . ."

Enough of that.

"All right, I get it," said Eric. "So before yesterday you couldn't smell?"

"I do not have a nose," she replied.

Makes sense.

"I have not yet received a body."

"But you could see and hear me?" Eric asked as he reached into the fridge and removed a jar of strawberry jelly and a tub of butter. "How does that work if you don't have eyes and ears?" *Boom. Gotcha.*

"Through our connection I can perceive the sights and sounds through your eyes and ears," she replied. *Dang she's good. Okay Ms. Answer-For-Everything.*

"But you can't perceive smell?" *Explain that.*

"Or touch either," she said. "I cannot explain it other than those things are not necessary for me to do my job."

Your job?

"And what is your job?" asked Eric. "To swoop in when a damsel in distress needs saving?"

Eric dipped the knife into the tub of butter and spread it across the warm toast. A new aroma wafted up into his nose, this time he paid special attention to it. *Now that smells nice.*

"It certainly does," agreed Maggie. "As for my job, I am tasked with recording, cataloging, and filing all of your unspoken thoughts."

Why?

"In the end, all must be accounted for."

He twisted the lid off the jar and dipped his knife into the dark red jelly.

I cannot wait to taste this, Maggie thought.

Eric slathered a healthy amount of jelly on the toast and licked the side of his finger where a remnant of strawberry had rubbed off the jar. Saliva pooled in his mouth beneath his tongue. *Tasty. Strawberry.* He walked around the counter to the living room side and sat on the lone stool opposite the sink. His stomach gurgled and growled as he lifted a piece of toast to his mouth. He took a bite and began to chew.

"Oh, oh that is wonderful," said Maggie. "Delicious. Oh I like that very much."

Geez.

"Are you going to do this for every bite?" asked Eric.

"Perhaps," said Maggie. "Elation is not a sin. You are meant to joy in life. There was a time when you reveled in a great many things."

Yeah when I was six.

"But then I grew up," he argued. "You can't go around oohing and aahing at every little thing." *Grown up.*

"And why not?"

Because people will think you are nuts.

Eric took another bite of his toast. *This is delicious though.*

"So what do we do now?" asked Eric. *What's the plan?*

"Well, the first thing you will need to do is get ready for work," replied Maggie.

Ugh. Work. Boo.

"Then we should probably talk about your date tonight."

Oh yeah, what are we going to do about that?

"Do you have any ideas?" he asked. *Might as well make yourself useful.*

"I have always wanted to try bowling," she replied. "It looks like such a joyous game."

No.

"Unless you are talking Wii bowling, then I'm out." *Nothing where I'll sweat.*

"Well then, what did you have in mind?" Maggie asked.

A movie.

"Dinner and a movie," he said definitively.

No, Maggie thought. *Something special.*

"You cannot talk during a movie," argued Maggie. "What about dinner and a walk through the park?"

That's actually pretty good. I like it.

"Sold!" he said. "Even better though, I think there is a free jazz concert in the park tonight."

"Perfect," Maggie said.

Girls like jazz, right?

Eric finished his toast and slid his plate into the sink. He looked up at the clock on the wall and grimaced. *Gotta get going. Work.*

"I was going to have some Lucky Charms," Eric said. "Do you think you can handle it or are you going to freak out every time I swallow a marshmallow?"

Perhaps, Maggie thought.

"I would like to try orange juice if we could," said Maggie.

Orange juice. That'll work.

"Sure," said Eric. "No problem."

Eric reached into the fridge and pulled out a red and orange container with a picture of Donald Duck on the side. He poured some juice into his Sacramento Kings glass and gulped it down. *Tangy.*

"Yes, that is very tangy," said Maggie. "Oh thank you. That is wonderful."

It kind of is.

All right, gotta go. He placed the glass in the sink and walked down the hall to the bathroom door. His feet left the carpet and landed softly on the tile floor.

I love the feel of the cold floor, Maggie thought.

He bent down and turned the water on in the shower. *How's this going to work?* Steam rose above the shower curtain and settled in a misty cloud on the bathroom ceiling. Eric looked into the mirror for a moment and then closed his eyes. Maggie felt him pull his shirt over his head and slip his pajama bottoms to the floor. He shook his feet free of his underwear and groped for the shower curtain with his eyes still closed.

What is he doing?

He stepped into the tub and the hot water pelted his feet.

That feels nice, thought Maggie.

"What are you doing, Eric?" Maggie asked. "Why are your eyes closed?"

"I don't want you to see me naked," replied Eric. *You're a girl. It's weird.*

"I have seen your mortal tabernacle nearly every day of your life," said Maggie.

Well that's horrifying. Peeping Maggie. I should really do more sit-ups. And who talks like that?

"Still, I'm more comfortable if you aren't peeping on me while you're in my head."

"Very well," she said. *What a peculiar thing to concern yourself with.*

Not sure how we'll handle when nature calls, Eric thought. *This is going to be awkward.*

With great care he moved his hands along the wet tiled wall until he brushed across the soap tray. He accidentally knocked the soap from the shelf with the back of his hand. It made a loud bang when it hit the bottom of the tub. *Shoot. Doggone it.* Maggie heard the bar slosh back and forth from end to end until it came to rest.

"Just open your eyes," Maggie pleaded. "It will be fine."

I bet you'd like that, you perv.

"I've got this," Eric bent over and felt around blindly until he grasped hold of the bar of soap. *Got it.* He opened his eyes momentarily to see a green bar in his hands near his feet.

"Uh oh," Maggie teased. "I saw your feet, oh the shame."

Stop that.

"All right, enough of that," Eric closed his eyes again and lathered the soap all over his body.

"It does feel nice to have a clean body, does it not?" Maggie said.

Ugh.

"Can you please not talk while I do this?" asked Eric. "It's just too weird."

"More weird than you washing yourself with your eyes closed?"

Yes.

"Very well," she said. "I will cease speaking until you are dressed."

"Thank you," Eric finished washing and clumsily placed the bar back in the tray. He turned off the water and pulled open the curtain. With his eyes still closed he leaned out of the tub and reached for the towel rack. As he pulled down on the towel he lost his footing on the slippery floor and tumbled out of the tub onto the fluffy floor mats in front of the toilet. *Ow.* Pulled free during his fall, the curtain rod came crashing down on his head.

Oh dear that does hurt quite a bit, Maggie thought. *This is unpleasant.*

This is the worst, Eric thought.

"Not a word," he said.

I would not dream of it, thought Maggie.

The Job

I'm in for it now. Eric walked into Bill's office and closed the door behind him.

"Have a seat." Bill gestured to the chair on the opposite side of his desk. *Hard chair. Principal's office.* Eric dutifully walked to the chair and sat down. A framed diploma hung over the credenza behind his manager's chair from Sacramento State University. Atop the credenza was a framed picture of Bill straddling a black Diavel Carbon Ducati with the American River behind him. *He is obsessed with that bike. I don't get it.* Next to the frame were a box of Kleenex and a bottle of hand sanitizer. *Germophobe.*

"So, tell me, what happened," said Bill. *Tell him you were sick.*

"Do not tell an untruth, Eric," chided Maggie.

Fine. But that's a double negative.

"A friend of mine needed me." Eric shifted in his chair. *This chair is the worst.*

"And you couldn't let me know?" asked Bill. *No time.*

"It was kind of an emergency," replied Eric. *Bright Eyes.*

"Just tell him, Eric," said Maggie. "Honesty is the best policy."

I am being honest.

"Honesty is not only truth telling, it is truth living," Maggie responded.

Are you some kind of Chinese fortune cookie? Give it a rest.

"You left your jacket, your keys, and your bag and just disappeared." Bill leaned forward in his chair and rested his elbows on his desk. "For all I knew you were kidnapped or dead." *Those were the only two options? What about fighting crime as a masked vigilante or hypnotized by an evil warlock? Have some imagination Bill.*

"I know," said Eric. "My bad." *Be contrite and let's get this over with.*

"What was so important that you went AWOL?" asked Bill. *AWOL? Is this the military?*

"Just tell him, Eric," said Maggie. "He will understand."

No he won't. Company man.

"It was Lindsey," Eric explained. "She got fired." *Stalin. Jerk.*

"Who's Lindsey?" asked Bill. *Oh right, you never leave your office. Loser.*

"Little Stalin's admin." Eric sat up straight in his chair. *A.K.A The best thing to ever happen to this place. Bright Eyes. Beautiful.* Maggie could feel his heart rate elevate slightly.

Love, she thought.

"What does that have to do with you?" asked Bill. *Everything. Nothing. I don't know.*

"She was crying," Eric answered. Bill tilted his head sideways and wrinkled his brow. *You know, crying? Like she was upset? Crying, you robot.* "In the rain. She was standing in the rain. Crying." *Have a heart, tin man.*

"And you, what?" asked Bill. "Took her an umbrella?" *That would have been helpful.*

"I took her to my place to get dry," he responded.

"Oh." Bill settled back into his chair and swiveled back and forth with raised eyebrows. *No, creep. Men are the worst.*

"It's not like that," argued Eric. "She needed somebody. It was a tough day. That's all."

"That may be so, but you can't just leave whenever you like," Bill responded. *Slave driver.*

"Make amends, Eric," urged Maggie.

Amends? You are so annoying.

"I'll make it up, I'll stay extra tomorrow," said Eric. *Will that make you happy?*

"That's not the point," said Bill. "I need to know where you are. There could have been a fire or a bomb threat and I'd have no idea if you got out safe or not." *A bomb threat? Who's going to bomb a candy dispensary? Kidnappings and bomb threats, this guy is paranoid and delusional. Be real.*

"Be submissive, Eric," said Maggie.

Is there a way to turn you off? Deactivate. Sleep. Heel. Bad girl. Bad.

"I understand," said Eric. "And I apologize. It won't happen again." *Unless she needs me.*

"You bet it won't, and you are going to stay late today and tomorrow." Bill stood up, walked around his desk and pulled open the door. *Today? No. Date. Bright Eyes.*

"I can't stay late today," said Eric. "I've got a date." *Eh, shouldn't have shared that.*

Bill stood in the doorway with his hand on his hip. "Let me guess, with Lindsey?"

"Yeah, and I can't break it," said Eric. "It's important, Bill." *More than important.*

"And what about your job?" asked Bill. "Is that important?" *No, it's just a stupid job.*

"Well, I would not say that," said Maggie.

What happened to honesty?

"If you are asking me to choose between this job and her," said Eric, "then I choose her."

Eric stood up from his chair and drew himself up straight. *Look taller.* He inhaled deeply and moved closer to Bill. The fluorescent light from the office space beyond bled into the subdued manager's office. *Don't blink.*

"Wow," said Bill. "You've really fallen for this girl, haven't you?" *Sure have. None of your business. Don't say a word. Are you prepared to quit? Yeah. Be strong.*

Bill stared down at him and partially blocked the doorway. *Your move, Hair Gel.*

"Relax," Bill finally added. "Nobody is asking you to choose between your job and a social life. You can make up the time tomorrow." *Hallelujah! Did not want to quit my job today. Not even sure she likes me yet. Bullet dodged.*

"Thanks, Bill," he said. *You're a decent guy.* Bill stepped to the side and Eric exited his office. *Free at last.*

"Just don't make a habit of this, okay?" Bill implored. *No worries. One time deal.*

Mark was at his desk with his back to them. He sat perfectly still and stared straight ahead at his monitor. *Eavesdropper. You're fooling no one.* Eric walked over and plopped into his desk chair. *Well this day is off to a terrific start.* He tapped on the keyboard and his monitor lit up. His wallpaper was a picture of Yoda wielding a green lightsaber. *Terrible that was. Could have been worse.* Bill stepped back into his office and closed the door behind him. *Finally.*

"Hey man, I tried to cover for you." Mark spun around in his chair the moment the door shut. *Who asked you to?*

"Eric, he is trying to be nice!" Eric jolted back as Maggie spoke. *What was that? Did you do that? Involuntary. Shocking.*

"I do not know," replied Maggie. *Did I?* she thought.

"Are you okay?" asked Mark. *I'm losing it.*

"Yeah, thanks, man," replied Eric.

"So what happened?" Mark leaned forward with a concerned look on his face. "Where did you run off to?" *Just summarize.*

"Lindsey got fired yesterday," he began. "She was upset and I saw her walking in the rain. We walked to my place to talk and dry off. That's all." *Oh and there is a voice in my head.*

"Wow, is she okay?" Mark asked. *I hope so.*

"I think so," replied Eric. *I'll find out tonight.*

The printer in the corner lit up and the rollers began to turn. A single sheet of white paper emerged out of the top and settled into the tray. *Saved by the printer.* Eric turned in his chair and began to stand up. Mark leapt from his seat and cut between Eric and the printer.

"Don't worry about that," Mark said. "I've got it. You take some time. Relax." *Relax?*

Mark retrieved the page from the printer and studied it for a moment. *What's the request?* He walked over to a box of white cables and picked one from the top. *Ah, network cable.* With the paper and cable in hand he moved to the door to the outside and opened it. He looked back at Eric and smiled before he stepped into the hallway. *He's a good dude. Annoying, but good.* The door closed and Eric sat in silence in the empty room. *Peace and quiet.*

"He does have a good heart," said Maggie.

And then it was gone.

"What was that herky jerky stuff?" asked Eric. *Possessed.* "Did you shock me or something?" *That was terrifying.*

"I am not sure," she replied. "I have heard of leapers fighting for control of their beholden's bodies." *Leapers?*

"What's a leaper?" he asked. *And what do you mean control?*

The door to Bill's office swung open and the wiry supervisor stepped into the room. *What now?* He looked at Mark's empty chair and then over to Eric.

"Who are you talking to?" asked Bill. *Cuss! Crazytown, population one.*

"Myself," Eric answered. *Eric, you moron, get it together.* Maggie felt warmth in his cheeks.

Bill grimaced and asked, "Where's Mark?"

"He's out on a service call," replied Eric.

"All right then," Bill said. "Salmen is calling about getting his new temp setup." *Already? Geez, she's been gone five minutes. No respect.*

"No, Bill," Eric protested. *No way. He can die for all I care.*

"Eric!" scolded Maggie.

You just hush.

"It's your job," Bill said calmly. *Come on.* "You can't let your personal stuff into it."

The guy is a jerk. He's the one who should be fired for being a tool. I hate him. Someone should knock his block off.

"Eric, please," said Maggie. "You are better than that. You must forgive so you can be free."

You are exhausting.

He exhaled deeply and placed his hands over his eyes.

"Fine," he conceded. "I'll do it."

"Oh good," said Maggie. "I am so pleased."

I was talking to Bill. I'll do the setup stuff not the forgiveness stuff.

Bill walked back into his office and moments later the printer lit up again and Eric retrieved the new page from the top tray. *Tiffany Truman. She'll never last.* He checked his pocket. *Phone. Check.* With a look over his shoulder at Bill's office he pulled open the door and walked out into the hall. *Keep it together.* He crinkled his nose. *Smell. Wax. Is somebody burning a candle? Is that legal in an office building? What is that smell? I'm sure it's a candle. Bizarre.* A short woman with blonde frizzy hair walked past him headed the opposite direction. *Irene. Accounting. The smell. It's her. Is that lotion? Candle scented lotion?*

"I think it smells lovely," said Maggie.

Yes, yes, everything is lovely.

Eric continued down the hall and out into the open office area. *What's a leaper?*

"A leaper is what we call someone who goes through the portal," Maggie explained.

So you are a leaper? It sounds slightly naughty.

A short bald man emerged from the cubicle at the end of the row. The glow from his bright red shirt reflected off his shiny head. *Carl.* He labored to remove a wrapper from a piece of candy and walked up the aisle without looking up. *Saved by the chocolate.* Eric turned the corner and headed for executive row.

"Yes, of a truth I am a leaper," said Maggie. "And yes, it is something that is forbidden."

Forbidden? You did something you were forbidden to do? How is that possible, Ms. Perfect?

"I am not perfect," she replied. *Fallen angel.* "I made a choice. My intentions are pure. I am at peace with my decision and am prepared to accept the consequences."

Consequences?

"What consequences?" asked Eric.

My turn, thought Maggie. With all that had transpired she had hardly had a moment to think beyond her present circumstances. She did not doubt that her actions had saved Lindsey's life and had possibly changed the course of Eric's. Her hope now was that her presence would not be a detriment to the remainder of Eric's days; days that she would not know for herself. She mourned a life that was over before it started—her life.

"Who are you talking to, Sugar?" Janice poked her head out of her cubicle and glanced up and down the row. *Ah! Stopping talking out loud, Nitwit.*

"Oh, um, just talking to myself," replied Eric with his cheeks again growing warm. *Come up with a better excuse.*

"Did you hear about Lindsey?" she asked in hushed tones. *Bright Eyes. Stalin. Rain.*

"Yeah," he muttered. *Tears. Towel. Hot cocoa.*

"Such a shame," Janice continued. "She was such a nice gal, really sweet." *Kind. Pretty.*

"Yeah." *Say something besides "Yeah."*

"Are you here to setup the temp?" *Tiffany. Next victim. Dead woman walking.*

Eric nodded and glanced over at Salmen's office. *Stalin. Jerk. Despicable.*

"It's not right the way he's allowed to treat people," said Janice. "I wish somebody would do something about it." *How does he get away with it? HR should fire him. It's so unfair.*

"Yeah, well, I'd better get to it," said Eric. *Before he has me fired too.*

He walked past the open door to Salmen's office. Inside the dimly lit room Salmen was hunched over his desk with his phone pressed to the side of his head, wearing his usual scowl on his mustached face. *What an unhappy soul.* Eric slipped around the column into Lindsey's former cubicle. He slid into the chair and rolled it closer to the desk. *It still smells like her.* On top of the desk was a bottle of lotion, a stack of multi-colored Post-It notes and a pen with faux sunflower on the end. *Sunflower. Even her pens are cute.* Patrick, a short young man with slicked back hair, approached the half wall counter. He stopped abruptly and stroked a thin patchy mustache. *Poser. Not now. Why me?*

"Where's the girl?" he asked. *The girl? You don't even know her name. I wish I didn't know your name, Patrick.*

"She was let go," replied Eric. *Fired. Tears. Rain. Bright Eyes.*

"Not surprised," Patrick replied nonchalantly. *You better watch yourself.* "I need him to sign this." *I don't care.*

"Well I'm not his admin." Eric pointed into the office and began typing on the keyboard. "I think he's on the phone." *So get lost. And shave that embarrassment above your lip.*

Patrick turned to look through the open door just as Salmen hung up the phone in a huff. *He even hangs up the phone like a jerk.* He emerged from his office like a mange bear from his cave and frowned at the loiterer across the hall.

"Hey boss." Patrick extended the papers he was holding. "I need your John Hancock on this bad boy." *Just say signature. Tool.*

"Eric, there is really no cause to think that way," said Maggie. "Ultimately, it is to your detriment and will do him no harm."

Give me a break, thought police.

Salmen took the papers from Patrick and placed them on the half wall counter next to Eric. He pulled out a pen and began to look over the document. *You smell like onions. Of course you do. Tiffany Truman. Log in. Check. Email? Check. All set.*

"So what happened to the girl?" Patrick asked as he leaned up against the outside of the cubicle. *Her name is Lindsey. Have some respect.*

"What?" Salmen asked with a distracted glance from the pages to Patrick. "Oh, she was just like the rest. Couldn't cut it."

Couldn't cut it? I'm gonna knock you out!

"Eric, do not entertain such thoughts," Maggie urged. "You cannot assault him."

Fine!

"You can't find good help these days, am I right?" Patrick responded. *You better watch yourself, you little suck up.*

"Eric, please," said Maggie. "I beg you."

I can't stand him.

"Yeah, they are all the same." Salmen signed the last page and handed the documents back to Patrick. "Pampered little girls who can't take the heat."

I'm going to punch him.

"Eric, you mustn't," she said.

Mustn't I?

"Temperance," Maggie implored.

You got the temper part right.

"She would cry at every little thing," Salmen continued. "Boohoo, the mean man asked me to do my job right. Whaaah." *That's it!*

Eric stood up from the desk and started around the column.

"He is not worth it, Eric," Maggie said. "You are better than this."

I'm really not.

He brushed past Patrick with a nudge of the shoulder.

Okay, fine. He's not worth it. He continued on without making eye contact with the mustached executive. *You coward. If you were a man you would have socked him in the mouth.*

"A real man knows when to walk away, Eric," said Maggie.

I'm a pretender.

"She did have a nice body though," Salmen remarked with a sneer. *Creep!*

"All right," said Maggie. "Punch him in the mouth."

Thank you.

"Gladly," said Eric. *The pain train's coming. Toot toot.*

He spun around and looked into the startled eyes of the duo loitering outside the cubicle. *You're going down. This is for Lindsey.* Without word and without warning he reached back and swung his fist forward as hard as he could. While the impact knocked Salmen to the floor, Eric's momentum pulled him off balance and he fell on top of his victim. *Ow. Have some, jerk. Geez that hurt.* Maggie felt an intense pain, followed immediately by a dull throbbing in Eric's hand. He quickly scrambled to his feet and stood over the fallen VP. *Stay down.* His heart pounded and he clinched his jaw.

"You are so fired," Patrick stated in disbelief.

You want a piece, brown nose? Eric's whole frame shook, his arms trembled and his body quaked. Maggie regretted her approval of such a violent action.

"Eric, no," cried Maggie.

I'm not going to hit him. Besides my hand hurts. Not doing that again. He is definitely not worth it. I think I broke my wrist.

"I quit," replied Eric. *Forget this place. I'm out.*

He strode away from the scene of the crime with a bounce in his step. *If ya smell what The Rock is cooking. Wish I had my own theme music. That would be epic.*

Church Boys

W*alk tall. Proud.* He squinted at the mid-morning sun, which, despite its brightness, offered no relief from the crisp winter air. Eric walked up the street with the Treat Mete building behind him growing smaller and smaller with each step. *Hope I didn't forget anything.* In his arms he carried an open copy paper box with an assortment of personal items thrown haphazardly together. On top were several candy dispensers that, until this morning, had lined the shelf above his desk. Beneath them were a stress ball and his favorite stapler. *Stapler thief. Mine. Rebel.* Lining the bottom of the box were several pictures displayed on his pegboard of his backpacking trip outside of Tahoe. *Trees. Mountains. Lake. Beautiful forest. Tent. Camping. I should probably get used to that since I'll be living in a tent soon. Unemployed.*

"Eric," Maggie began.

Not now. Seriously, just give it a rest.

"Eric," she continued. "Perhaps you could return and apologize."

I'm not sorry. Forget him and forget that place. I'd do it again. Long time coming.

"Very well," said Maggie. "Then what are we going to do now?"

We? I am going to go home and take a nap. Midday naps are the best. I might ice my hand. You can do what you like.

He stopped momentarily to adjust his grip on the box. As he did, a clear glass plaque slid to one side. *Award.* Eric reached in and pulled it from the pile of his possessions. The white lettering etched into the glass read "Employee of the Quarter: Eric Barkley Q3 2013." *Before April. I used to care. Heartless. What have I done?*

"Poop," he muttered. *Oh man. I'm hosed. What am I going to do now?*

"May I offer a suggestion?" asked Maggie.

No.

"No you may not," Eric said. *No suggestions. No advice. And no more nagging. Please.*

Eric dropped the plaque back in the box and continued up the road. Traffic in the quasi-residential neighborhood was steady but orderly. *Why are so many people driving around? Don't these people have jobs?* One by one vehicles moved through the intersection, alternating in a counterclockwise direction. *Maybe they all got fired too. Or quit. We quit. I mean I quit.* The driver in a black Mercedes waiting at the stop sign waved him along and Eric hustled between the thick white lines of the crosswalk. *Bet that guy has a good job. Nice ride.* The contents of the box bounced around with each bounding step. *Careful. Oh who cares? I don't care about any of this junk.* Maggie felt his body pull to his right as he jostled the box back and forth. There was a dulled burning sensation in his biceps as he labored on toward his destination. *Seriously, I need to work out. At least now I'll have the time. Ba da bum.* It felt to Maggie as if his heart sank at the thought.

As he turned onto his street, the beaming sun was at his back. *Relief. I need to get some new shades. Crow's feet.* At the far end of the lane he saw two well-dressed young men in dark suits. *Salesmen? Don't want any.* Even from a distance he could see the smiles on their faces. *Oh no. Mormons. Not them. Not now.*

Hear them.

"Did you feel that?" asked Maggie.

Quiet you.

Eric quickened his steps. *You can make it. Walk faster.* He caught sight of his front door, equidistant between himself and the suited young men. *You're not gonna make it. Maybe they'll pass by. Don't make eye contact.* He looked down at the sidewalk.

"Hi," said one of the young men. *Shoot. Now what? Just keep walking.*

"Hey," Eric replied as he skirted past them on the far side of the sidewalk.

Hear them.

"Eric?" the young man said. *What? How? No way.*

He looked up into the smiling faces of the two missionaries he had met in the Raley's parking lot. *They remembered my name.* He stopped next to them and adjusted his box.

"It's Eric, right?" the young man asked. *Uh, yeah. Think fast.*

Eric looked down at the black name tag on the young man's coat pocket. *Elder Harper.*

"Elder Harper," he said. *Funny name.*

Elder Harper stuck out his hand. *Shake.*

"You have a good memory." *Nope.*

"I read it on your badge there," said Eric gesture toward his chest. *I can read.*

"Right," Elder Harper smiled. "How are you?" *Unemployed.*

"Busy," Eric said as he stepped backwards away from them.

Be still.

"You are not busy, Eric," argued Maggie. "And you are ignoring a prompting again."

No, I'm ignoring you.

"We understand," said Elder Harper. "Eric, tell me, do you believe in God?" *Yeah, I guess.*

"Sure," replied Eric. *How do you say no to that?*

"So do I," Elder Harper continued. "We are here because we have a message from God for you. It's a message of hope and peace. It is that God lives and He sent His Son for us that we might return to live with Him." *Return?*

"What do you mean 'return'?" asked Eric. *Return to where?*

"We lived with God before we were born," Elder Harper said.

You lived with God before you were born.

"You mean like as spirits?" asked Eric. "You believe that?" *Spirits. Maggie.*

"Yes I do," Elder Harper replied with a smile. *Why don't I remember that?*

"Ask them," Maggie implored. "They are here to answer your questions."

Okay, fine. Let's see what they've got.

"Does your church have exorcists?" asked Eric. *Possessed. Spirit. Annoying.*

"Eric!" exclaimed Maggie.

What? I'm just making conversation.

"Do you need an exorcist?" Elder Harper asked with a nervous chuckle. *Maybe.*

"Eric, those are not the questions I meant and you know it," chided Maggie.

I'm just trying to help. Maybe they can help you return, ya know.

"No, probably not," Eric replied. *Are you happy? No exorcist.* "I was just curious if you've ever heard spirits coming here early, like before they are supposed to." *Is that better?*

Maggie felt Eric's muscles strain against the box and a throbbing pain in his wrist. *This is heavy.* His fingers slipped and he braced the bulk of the weight with his hip and shifted his hands beneath the box. *Much better. Home. I've got to set this thing down. Need an exit excuse. Think.*

"Can we help you with that?" asked the suited young man next to Elder Harper. *Name.* The shoulder strap from his bag covered half of his black name tag. *Elder something.*

"No I'm good, Elder . . . ?" *Probably Smith.*

"Sorry," he said moving the strap away from his tag. "I'm Elder Anders." *Anders. Harper. Why are you trying to remember their names?*

"It's no trouble." Elder Anders said as he reached out and took the box from Eric. *No. I've got it. Come on. Okay, maybe I'll let him hold it for a minute.*

"Where are you headed?" asked Elder Harper. *Home.*

"Back to my place," said Eric. *Shoot, now they're gonna ask where you live.*

"Oh yeah, where do you live?" asked Elder Anders. *Called it.*

Eric turned to his left and glanced back at the door of his condo. *Might as well invite them in, it's the polite thing to do.*

"Yes, Eric," said Maggie. "We should invite them to stay and talk."

We? How about me, or I? Any way I'm just inviting them in so we can discuss more about getting rid of pesky spirits.

"I'm just right over there," Eric said with a gesture back and behind him. "You want to come in and rest or something? You must be tired from walking around all day."

"Thanks," Elder Harper said. "We have an appointment but we can help you get your box home." *An appointment? An appointment for what? I thought these guys just knocked on doors and rode bicycles. I can carry the box twenty more feet. Oh well.*

Eric led the trio up the walkway to his front door. With a turn of the key he opened the door and stepped to the side to usher in his visitors. *Come on in.* Elder Harper entered followed by Elder Anders, who still carried Eric's box. *What do church people drink?*

"You can just set that down anywhere," Eric said. "Can I get you something to drink?"

Elder Anders sat the box down on the floor and began studying Eric's collectible AT-AT. *I bet he's a Star Wars fan. Who isn't? Oh right, Lindsey. Bright Eyes.*

"We're all right," replied Elder Harper. "This is a nice place you have here." *Thanks.*

"It's nothing fancy but it's home," answered Eric. *For now. Homeless. Jobless.*

Almost on cue the heater kicked on and warm air poured out of the vent. *Heavenly.*

Oh that is nice, thought Maggie. *I do like the warmth.*

"It's way nicer than the dinky little apartment we live in," said Elder Anders.

"So you guys live together?" asked Eric as he climbed up on the stool by the kitchen counter. "Please have a seat." *If you're staying.*

"Yep," replied Elder Harper. "Not far from here actually." *Are they from here?*

"So are you guys from around here?" he asked. *I thought you all came from Utah.*

"Nope, we're from Utah," replied Elder Harper. *I knew it!*

"That's cool," Eric said. "So did you come out here together?" *Like the Peace Corps.*

"Actually, Anders is from southern Utah and I'm from Salt Lake City," replied Elder Harper as he sat down on the futon. "We've only know each other for about two weeks." *Interesting.*

"And now you live together?" he asked. *I could never do that. Stranger danger. No thank you. Too many weirdos out there. And Dave.*

"We'll serve together for a couple months and then we'll get a new companion or move to a new area," explained Elder Anders as he turned his attention from the AT-AT and looked up at the Braveheart poster on the wall. *Such a strange life. Why?*

"Do you ever get assigned to live with a girl missionary?" he asked. *That would be a great reality TV show. I'd watch.*

"No, elders server with elders and sisters with sisters," answered Elder Harper with a look at the used Star Wars mug that still sat on the arm of the futon where Lindsey left it. *Bummer.*

"So you are a Star Wars fan." *Sure am.*

"Yeah," replied Eric. "You?" *If he says no I'm throwing him out.*

"Eric!" said Maggie. "You will not."

Relax. I'm only joking, mostly.

"I love Star Wars," said Elder Harper. "My whole family does. Two years ago for Halloween we dressed up like a family of Wookies, all of us: my dad, my mom, my two brothers and my sister and me." *That's amazing. Big family. So cool.*

"That's so cool," said Eric. *If I ever have kids, we are so doing that.*

"So where do you work?" asked Elder Anders. *Punch. Fired. Quit.*

"Actually, I just quit my job today," Eric replied. "I used to work at Treat Mete, a candy dispenser manufacturer." *Stalin. Bright Eyes. Worth it.*

"That's why you were carrying the box," replied Elder Harper. *Yep.*

"Yeah," Eric replied. *Change the subject.* "So do you guys have jobs or do you do this all day?" *That's not a subject change, more of an attention change. It works.*

"We do this all day every day," Elder Harper said with a big smile. *He's a happy one, isn't he? What's the deal with that?*

"How do you live?" asked Eric. *Food. Rent. Clothes.*

"We volunteer to serve as missionaries for two years," Elder Harper explained. "I saved up money while I was in high school and my family helps some." *Two years? Unbelievable!*

"Two years?" Eric shook his head. *That's crazy.* "What made you want to get into missionarying?" *Missionarying? Is that a word? Come on, Eric, you sound ignorant.*

The elders look at each other and laughed.

"Partly because we're expected to serve," Elder Anders replied. "But I came out because I wanted to show my love for my Heavenly Father and my Savior." *Wow. Who talks like that?*

Maggie felt a swelling in Eric's chest.

Warm. What is that about?

"So do you guys date or anything?" Eric asked. *Lindsey. Bright Eyes. Beautiful.*

"Not as missionaries," Elder Harper replied. "Anders here has a girlfriend back home, but we do not date for two whole years." *That's probably smart. Maybe I should be a missionary. Less anxiety, less stress.*

"Do you have a girlfriend?" asked Elder Anders. *No. Maybe. I hope. Bright Eyes.*

"I wouldn't call her that," said Eric. "But there is this girl. We have a date tonight." *She's the one. I want to show my love for her. Now he's got me talking like that.*

"What's her name?"

"Lindsey," replied Eric. Maggie felt his heart beat faster. *Bright Eyes.*

"Where are you going on your date?" *Good question.*

"I was thinking dinner and a walk in the park," he replied. *Classy.*

"YOU were thinking?" Maggie said.

Fine, we were thinking. Happy?

"Nice," said Elder Harper. "Where are you going to eat?" *Why? Are you two gonna follow me? Don't answer. Be vague.*

"Not sure yet," Eric shifted on top of the stool. *Change the subject.* "You sure I can't get you guys a drink?" *Water. OJ. Water. You need to go shopping.*

"No, thank you," Elder Harper said. "We've really got to run." *Appointment.*

"All right," Eric stood up and walked toward the front door. "Thanks for the hand." *Hand. My hand. Hurt. Punch. Mistake.*

"Eric," Elder Harper began. "Like we said, we share a message of hope and we'd love to come back and talk with you more. Would that be okay?" *Hope. Jobless. Lindsey.*

Hear them.

"I don't know," Eric began. *Lindsey.*

Hear them.

"You guys are welcome to drop by but I'm gonna be busy looking for a job and things." *Just tell them no.*

Hear them.

"Totally understand," said Elder Harper. "What kind of work did you say you did?" *I didn't, did I? Computers. IT.*

"I work in IT doing desktop support," Eric pulled open the door. *Mr. Fix-It. Cathy. Stalin. Good riddance. Bill. Mark. I'm gonna miss it there. What am I saying?*

"No kidding," replied Elder Harper. "My dad owns a tech support company." *Is he hiring?*

"Oh yeah," Eric leaned against the door. "Does he do business in Sacramento?" *Probably not. Worth a try.*

"No, it's mostly local businesses," he replied with a wink. "You want to move to Salt Lake?" *Uh, no. Snow. Cold. Mormons. Pass.*

"I don't think so," Eric replied. *No chance.*

"Well if we hear of anything we'll let you know," Elder Harper and Elder Anders stepped out onto the front porch.

Hear them.

"I'd appreciate it," Eric said.

Hear them.

"You know what, if you guys are in the neighbor and catch me at home, I'll listen to what you have to say." *I'll throw them a bone. Establish boundaries though.* "I'm not joining your church or anything, but I'll listen." *Anybody who would dress like a Wookie with his family can't be all bad.*

"It's a deal," Elder Harper extended his hand and Eric shook it. *He's got a good grip.*

The elders turned and headed up the walkway toward the street. *Nice guys.* Eric closed the door and looked down at the box of stuff on the floor. *Jobless. What now? Date. Lindsey.*

"I really like those boys," said Maggie.

Of course you do. Church boys.

First Date

A chill swept down Eric's spine when he met with a cold winter breeze as he turned the corner onto L Street. *Brrr.* His shoulders wriggled uncontrollably and he pulled at the collars of his jacket. *Cold neck.*

"That felt extraordinary," said Maggie. "Wow, I mean it was exhilarating."

Calm down.

"It felt flipping cold," responded Eric. "Are you going to keep freaking out over every little thing?" *Toast. Rain. Shampoo. Doorknobs. Wind. It's getting ridiculous.*

"These are not little things," Maggie argued. "Life is incredible. You should savor every part of your mortal journey."

You are exhausting. I don't have the energy.

"And for the record, shampoo is miraculous." Maggie added.

"I'm done talking to you now," he said. *Her place is just up here so let's keep the crazy to a minimum. As if that were possible.*

"But I can still talk to you, right?" she asked.

I wish you wouldn't. This is hard enough.

He turned up a narrow concrete walkway that led between two sets of buildings. *301.* On the building to his left the numbers 101–104 were displayed on a small plaque in the upper corner. The plaque on the building to his right read 201–204. He continued up the walkway to the second set of buildings and turned left toward a maroon door with the numbers 301 above a small peep hole. *This is it. Go time.*

"Are you going to tell her you were fired?" asked Maggie.

I quit. And no, I don't think I'll open with that.

Eric pulled his phone from his pocket and checked the time. *7:00 p.m.* He inhaled slowly, reached up and knocked on the door. *Breathe. Be cool. Look cool. Cool but not disinterested. Look interested. But not creepy guy interested. Just look normal. What's normal though?*

"Relax, Eric," said Maggie. "It will all be okay."

How do you know? Can you see the future? If you can see the future, you better tell me. Do I go bald? Please tell me I don't go bald.

"I cannot see the future," replied Maggie. "I just meant, 'have faith.' "

Faith. Right.

He looked back toward the street as a couple passed in the distance. Dusk had settled over the quiet neighborhood and the automatic streetlights clicked on. *Is she home?* He leaned toward the door. *I don't hear anything. Knock again?* In the doorframe to his right was a small round button. *Doorbell. Push it.* He reached out and pressed it gently with his index finger. *Ding dong. What if she heard the knock? Now you look impatient. What now? You can't take it back. This is a horrible start.* He stepped away from the door and put his hands behind his back. *Look patient. How do you look patient, idiot? Keep it together. I still don't hear anything. Is she home? Did she forget? Is she hurt?*

Maggie began to worry too.

"Knock again, Eric," she said.

No way. I already knocked AND rang the doorbell.

"She could be hurt,' said Maggie.

Or she could be getting ready or she could not even be home. Or she's home and she doesn't want to see me. This is the worst night of my life.

"Calm down," Maggie pleaded.

Calm down? You just said she could be hurt.

"What if she is?" Maggie replied. "What are you going to do?"

Knock again.

He hesitated a moment and reached up to knock again when he heard the soft sounds of steps approaching the door. *Wait. Someone is there.* Quickly he backed away from the door and put his hand in his pocket. *Be cool.* The lock clicked and the doorknob jiggled before the door opened slowly. *Here we go.* Lindsey stood in the doorway with a grin and a nod. She wore a peach turtleneck sweater and a pair of blue jeans. *She looks amazing.*

"Hi," said Eric. *Hi? That's the best you can do? At least you didn't say hey'll.*

"Hi," Lindsey responded cheerily. *Bright Eyes. I could hear that hi the rest of my life.*

"Tell her she looks nice," interrupted Maggie.

I was going to. Pipe down, you.

"You look nice," said Eric. *Are you happy? You ruined the moment.*

"Thank you." Lindsey smiled and looked down at the floor.

"My apologies," said Maggie. "I will remain silent."

Thank you.

"Are you ready?"

"Yes, just one second." Lindsey stepped back inside and turned off the lamp in the front room. She retrieved her purse from the floor next to the door and checked it for her keys. "Ready." *Great.*

As she closed the door behind her a gray mangy cat sauntered up beside her and rubbed against her leg. *Ew. Cat hair.* Lindsey reached down and stroked its head briefly before she walked over to stand next to Eric. *Cat lady. I thought she said she wasn't a pet person.*

"Is that yours?" he asked as they strode down the walkway toward the street. *Please say no.*

"No," she said. "It's just a cat from the neighborhood. Do you like cats?" *No.*

"I hate cats," he said. "I'm allergic." *We've got something in common; we're both allergic to something. Peanut butter. Cat hair.*

She folded her arms and looked down at the ground *Uh oh. She's upset. What did I say? Oh man, she probably loves cats. Just look at the way she pet it. Way to go, Eric.* They continued to walk in silence as they turned up the sidewalk and headed down L Street. *Say something.*

"Can I say something?" asked Maggie.

No.

You can fix this. Think, man. They continued to walk up the oak-lined lane for nearly a block before Lindsey looked up, took in a deep breath and cleared her throat.

"I don't understand how or why people hate a thing," she said as her voice cracked slightly. "It didn't ask to be. It's just here, like you and me. It was created and it just is. I don't see the point in hating it."

"Some things have earned the hate," he answered. *Bullies. Little Stalin. Justin Beiber.*

"And what do you get for your hate?" Lindsey turned and met his gaze. *Bright Eyes. She's right. What is wrong with you, Eric? Beautiful inside and out. Kind. Loving. Caring.*

"Dunno, sometimes you just want to hurt back at something that hurt you," he replied. *It sounds petty when I say it out loud. I hope she doesn't think we're still talking about cats.*

They reached the corner and Eric gestured to turn right. The silence was broken only by the occasional passing car. In the distance they heard the growing rumble of conversation and could see a line of bright yellow lights hanging from a wire. *Talk to her.*

"Do you like Italian food?" he asked. *If she says no I'm going to jump into oncoming traffic.*

"Yes, I do." *Thank heavens.*

"Good deal," he said. "There's a bistro right up here that has the best chicken parm. Have you been there?" *April. Heartless. Date. Angel hair.*

"No I haven't," she replied. *Oh right, new girl in town.*

"I think you'll like it," said Eric. *I hope you will.*

She smiled and nodded. The smell of fresh baked bread wafted out onto the street as they passed in front of the bistro. *Yum. Breadsticks.*

"Oh, that is delightful," Maggie said. "Can we get some breadsticks? I would so love to try them."

They come with your meal and they are amazing. You'll love them. I love them. We'll love them? I'm not sure how this works.

Eric ushered Lindsey through a waist-high iron gate and up to the hostess desk.

"How many?" a perky brunette behind the desk asked with a smile. *She's happy to be here.*

"Two," replied Eric. *That's right, we're together.*

"Inside or outside? There's no waiting for outside and we have heat lamps," said the hostess.

Eric turned to Lindsey. "Do you have a preference?"

"Not really," she replied. "Outside is fine." *She's easygoing. I like that. No waiting.*

"Outside will be fine," he said to the hostess.

The brown-haired hostess collected a pair of menus and utensils rolled up in napkins and led the way to a small circular table along the decorative iron fence that bordered the restaurant. *Be a gentleman.* Eric pulled out Lindsey's chair and waited for her to be seated. He then took his place opposite her on the other side of the table. The menus and napkins were placed in front of them. *Let's hear the specials.*

"Our special tonight is Penne with Chicken or Sausage. April will be your server. We'll get some breadsticks out to you right away," the bubbly brunette turned and bounced away. *April. Couldn't be. Could it? Nah.*

Eric smiled across the table and opened his menu. Lindsey removed her utensils from the cloth napkin and placed them on the table before she laid the napkin across her lap. *You should do that too. Be classy.* Eric unrolled the napkin and the fork and knife clanked off the edge of the table and unto the floor. *Cuss. Smooth move.* He bent over quickly to retrieve the silverware. A pair of black shoes appeared and came to a stop near the leg of the iron table.

"Hi, I'm April," said the voice belonging to the shoes. *I know that voice.* "I'll be your server tonight. Oh, let me get you a new set of silverware, sir." *This isn't happening.*

He slowly looked up from her shoes to her black slacks and shirt to her blue eyes and blonde hair. *NOOOOOOOOOOO!*

"Eric?" the blonde server exclaimed. *Heartless. April. Brad. Carnations.*

"Oh dear," cried Maggie.

Cuuuuuuuuuuss.

"April, what are you doing here?" he asked. *Why me?*

"I work here," replied April. *You've got to be kidding me.*

"Since when?" *Just my luck.*

"I started a few months ago," she replied. *Why here?* "It's good to see you." *It is?*

"Yeah," he mumbled. *What is happening? Is this real? Twelve months! Twelve months and now this. Why?*

"How have you been?" she asked. *Good, say good.*

"I've been good," he replied. "You?" *I don't care.*

"Good," she said with a vigorous head nod. *You look good.*

"You look good." *Why did you say that? Ah!*

"Is this your girlfriend?" she asked. *Oh crud, Lindsey. Quick, fix this.*

"Oh, um, yeah, I mean, no," he stammered. "This is Lindsey. She's . . . we, um, we're on a date." *This is a disaster! I wish that heater would just fall on me right now.*

He looked over at Lindsey who sat with her hands in her lap and watched them.

"Hi, Lindsey," she said warmly. *Don't be so nice. You are a cold-blooded harpy.*

"Pleased to meet you," Lindsey replied. *She is so sweet. What am I going to do?*

"Eric used to bring me here too," said April. *NO! Stop talking.* "It's the reason I'm working here now, I love the food so much I thought why not work here?" *Of course. This is all my fault. We should not have come here. Grab Lindsey and run.*

"What happened to Macy's?" asked Eric. *Did they fire you for hooking up with your boss?*

"Brad and I broke up," she explained. *Ha ha.* "I moved on." *Serves you right.*

"Eric, to wish ill on others only does you harm," said Maggie. "Did you not listen to Lindsey?"

Okay. You're right. My bad.

"I'm sorry to hear that." *No I'm not.*

"Eric!" chided Maggie.

Last one, I promise.

"Que sera sera, right?" April replied. *More like what goes around comes around.*

"Right." *I don't think I can take much more of this. Yell fire and get Lindsey out of here.*

"Can I get you started with something to drink?" she asked and looked over at Lindsey.

"Oh, I'll just have a water," said Lindsey. *Get what you like, I'm buying.*

"Got it," April said. "And do you still drink Diet Coke with a lemon wedge?" *She remembered. Wow. What does that mean?*

"Nah, I'll have a water too," he replied. *That's right, I've changed. You don't know me. I do want a Diet Coke with a lemon wedge though. Dang it, she's ruining everything.*

"A lemon wedge would be nice though," interjected Lindsey. *We both like lemon wedges in our drink, that's got to mean something. Meant to be.*

"Sure thing, honey," replied April. *Don't call her honey.* "Two waters with lemon wedges. I'll be right back with some bread sticks." *If I choke on a breadstick maybe I can wake up from this nightmare.*

She walked away from the table and Lindsey sat back in her chair and stared at the menu. *What is she thinking? Is she upset?* Eric tapped at his menu with his pinky finger and forced a smile on his face. *This is so awkward.*

"So you two dated?" Lindsey asked. *Come clean, there's no getting around it.*

"Yeah, but we broke up a year ago," Eric said. "Actually she broke up with me. It was pretty terrible." *Why did you say that? Over-share. She doesn't care.*

"I'm sorry." *Great, now she pities you.*

"Oh, that is sarcasm," Maggie said. "Because it is not great for her to pity you." *Ugh. Yes. Bravo. Now be quiet, please.*

"Don't be," Eric said. "It was for the best." *I would rather be with you.*

"She's very pretty," said Lindsey. *It's a trap!*

"Not so much on the inside though." *Truth.*

"Oh?" *Don't elaborate.*

"She had me meet her in the park, where she broke up with me, standing beside her new boyfriend." *Why did you share that? Come on, man.*

"Yikes," said Lindsey. *Indeed.*

"Yeah, and to top it off I brought flowers." *Pink carnations.*

"Here are your breadsticks." The brunette hostess returned with a basket full of golden brown pieces of bread. Steam rose up from the basket and the aroma permeated the table.

"That smell is incredible!" said Maggie.

Not now.

"Right, sorry. You are in the middle of something."

Ya think?

"Thank you," Lindsey said. When the hostess was gone they both sat in silence and looked at the bread. *Offer her a breadstick.*

"I'm afraid I wasn't honest with you," Lindsey said as she looked at the basket. *Oh boy.*

"Really?" *What could it be? She loves cats. She's actually seen Star Wars. She's in the witness protection program.*

"Yeah, I don't really like Italian food," she admitted. *That's it? What a relief.*

"Me neither!" Eric excitedly sat up in his chair. *Tomatoes. Bleh.*

"Then why did you bring me here?" asked Lindsey with an amused look on her face.

"Because I wanted to take you some place fancy," said Eric. "This is the fanciest place I know. Plus eating at a bistro sounds sophisticated and I thought you might be into it."

"But you said you like the chicken parmesan?" *True.*

"It's the only thing on the menu that I'll even eat," he replied. "And the breadsticks. Those things are addicting." *Mmmm, breadsticks.*

"So you think I'm the sophisticated type?" asked Lindsey. *Yeah. You read books and stuff.*

"Aren't you?" *Are you?*

"Not really," she smiled. *Super. Let's bounce.*

"There's this little dive taco shop around the corner," he said. "You wanna get out of here?"

"I sure do." She threw her napkin on the table and grabbed her purse. *This girl is amazing.*

"But the breadsticks," cried Maggie. "Can we not try just one?" *Forget the breadsticks. You'll love tacos, I promise.* "I am certain I will, but could we not have both?" *Greedy.*

Eric stood up and leapt over the small iron fence out onto the sidewalk. He turned around and extended his hand toward Lindsey. She took hold of it and he pulled her out of her chair. *Her hand is so soft.* Maggie could feel the energy flow through his body from her touch. She stepped up onto the brick foundation and hopped over the fencing. *Now this is fun.* They both laughed as they shuffled around the corner and out of sight. *Bye-bye April.*

***

"What do you think?" he asked. *Please like it.*

Lindsey had a mouth full of taco and held up her finger while she chewed. *She's got her mouth full, relax, Eric. She's smiling though. That's good.* After she had swallowed she reached for a paper napkin on the picnic table between them. She held it over her mouth.

"It's really good," replied Lindsey. *Sweet! She likes it.* "Kind of greasy though." *Shoot! She hates it. She doesn't "hate" anything, remember? Right. Well, she thinks it's greasy.*

"Yeah, but so good," said Eric. *Greasy meat. Greasy cheese. Greasy good.*

"So good," she agreed before taking another bite. *Even her chewing is cute.*

The fluorescent lighting illuminated a large red and white menu painted on the wall next to a pickup window. Above the menu were the cursive letters "Javy's Tacos." Lindsey and Eric sat under a metal awning on a wire metal picnic table set with rubberized covering over the mesh pattern. Outside of the napkin dispenser, the only thing that adorned the table was the wax paper wrappers their tacos had been enclosed in. *This is more my style.*

"That is good, Eric," said Maggie. "Just be yourself."

You're right. What have I got to lose? If she doesn't like me then I'll just be alone forever with the voice in my head.

"Was that sarcasm too?" asked Maggie.

What do you think?

"So was Brad the boyfriend at the park?" asked Lindsey. *Brad. Park. Pink carnations.*

"Yeah," Eric sighed. "He was her boss at Macy's. She said she didn't intend for it to happen but they had more in common." *Enough about your sad tale. Change the subject.*

"Dating people at work is never a good idea," Lindsey joked. *Nice one. I love this girl.*

"Well we don't have to worry about that anymore," Eric replied with a wink and a grin.

The smile fell from Lindsey's face and she took a hasty bite of her taco. *Uh oh. That was the wrong thing to say.* She looked down at the table and chewed slowly. *Fix this.*

"I'm sorry," he said. "I didn't mean that. I meant to say that we don't work together anymore. That is neither of us work there now, actually." *That was clumsy.*

"What do you mean?" She held the napkin over her mouth while she spoke. *Hero story.*

"I mean I quit today," he replied. "Or I was fired. I'm not exactly sure what came first. I punched Salmen in the face and walked out." *Heroic. That's just the kind of guy I am.*

"You didn't!" she exclaimed. "I hope you didn't do that for me." *She's upset? Shoot.*

"Well no, I mean, kinda." *This was not the reaction I expected.*

"Oh Eric, you didn't." She dropped her taco on the table and buried her head in her heads.

"I sure did," said Eric. *Be confident. Own it.* "He's a creep and he had it coming. You're a good person and you didn't deserve that." *He's a piece of garbage and you're an angel.*

"You don't know anything about me," she argued. *I do too.*

"I know who you are," said Eric. "If I knew nothing more than that you care for a ratty old cat that's not even yours and when you smile my heart feels like it's going to burst, that would be enough." *I love you.*

"Tell her Eric," said Maggie.

Too soon.

"It's never too soon," Maggie argued.

I beg to differ.

Lindsey took another bite of her taco but stared out and away at the concrete curb. *Okay it's awkward again. Let's just eat.* Eric glanced up frequently as he devoured his tacos. *What to say now?* He pulled a napkin from the dispenser and wiped his greasy mouth and fingers. He put the soiled napkin on the table and cleared his throat. *Lighten the mood. Make a joke. Be funny.*

"So where would we need to eat in Redding to run into one of your old boyfriends?" he joked. *Nice one. Clever.*

Lindsey's face changed from solemn to troubled. *Uh oh.* She did not look up at him but stood up and folded her arms uncomfortably. *This is it. It's over.* Eric stood up slowly and looked intently over at his date. *Nice move, dummy.*

"It's getting late," Lindsey said. *It's 8:15.* "Thank you for the tacos. They were delicious." *Don't do this. Don't push me away. I'm sorry.*

"Lindsey," Eric began. "I . . ."

"It's okay," she interrupted. "I'm just very tired." *Okay.*

"All right," Eric conceded. "Let me walk you home." *Don't give up man.*

They left the fluorescent lights of Javy's Taco Shop behind them and stepped out into the dark streets. *Say something. Tell her how you feel. Don't let her go.* A cold breeze blew a large group of leaves, which passed by entirely unconcerned with the silent duo. To Maggie, this wind seemed colder than the first and not exhilarating at all. *No way. Is that the cat?* In the distance Eric spotted a small silhouette of a cat beneath the streetlight. It trotted toward them and sauntered between Lindsey's legs. *It did not ask to be created.* Eric reached down and petted the cat on the top of its head. His hand vibrated as it purred softly. *You're not so bad.* He looked up at Lindsey and she smiled at him. *There's that smile.*

"Ah-choo," Eric sneezed loudly. *Doggone allergies.*

Lindsey giggled as the cat scampered through the hedges into the neighboring yard. *My eyes are itching. Worth it. Don't rub them.* They continued down the lane. All at once their surroundings seemed brighter to Maggie and not as heavy as they had been just moments earlier. *Talk to her. Jazz. Ask her if she likes jazz.*

"I'm not a good person," said Lindsey, breaking the silence. *Of course you are.*

"Why do you say that?" asked Eric. "You are kind, caring, and decent. I don't think there are additional qualifications." *If you are not a good person, then no one is.*

"You won't find a boyfriend in Redding," she said. "You'll find a trail of broken lives that all lead back to me." *Yikes.*

"I'm sure that's not true," argued Eric. *No way.*

"It is," Lindsey shot back. "It is true." *Tell me. It won't matter. I promise.*

"Eric, I think you should trust her," said Maggie. "You may not like what you hear."

What do you know, Maggie? Do you know what she is talking about?

"I believe I do," she confirmed.

Tell me.

"It is not mine to tell," said Maggie.

You're right. I want to hear it from her.

There was a low rumble from the patrons on the patio of the bistro. *Back to where we started.* They stood on the corner as a black sedan rolled to a stop at the intersection. *Don't look over. April. Heartless. Dine and dash.* The sedan continued straight and they crossed the street to the other side. As they turned left, Lindsey shifted and looked over at Eric. *Go on.*

"My older sister had a boyfriend," she began. "He was the captain of the football team and everyone in town worshipped him. He had a full ride scholarship to Cal. He was handsome and smart. To me he seemed to hold the world in his hand. He had everything and anything he wanted."

She choked up and wiped a tear from her eye. *What did he do to you?*

"I was thirteen, I didn't know anything about men," she continued. "He just made me feel so good. He paid attention to me. Me, of all people. I knew it was wrong but I didn't stop it." *Oh no. No way. He didn't.*

"When he went to jail," she went on and her expression hardened and her voice turned cold, "my sister said that I ruined his life and hers. My father was ashamed of me and hasn't looked at me since. At school I was the slut who killed the hopes and dreams of an entire community." *What do I say?*

They continued down the sidewalk. The leaves rustled in the large oak canopies above them. *Tell her it's okay. Tell her he was a creep.*

"You still think I'm a good person?" she asked. *Yes.*

Eric caught her by the arm and they stopped in the shadow of a massive oak tree.

"Yes I do," he said emphatically. "What he did was inexcusable. You were a child. The law and society requires that he be punished. You didn't do that to him. He did. You didn't do that to your sister. He did. I don't know your dad, but any man who would turn his back on his daughter is a schmuck. And I couldn't give two craps about what a bunch of high school kids in Redding think. Lindsey Jackman, you are a good person. Believe that." *And I love you.*

She burst into tears with Eric still holding onto her arm.

Hold her.

He stepped toward her and wrapped his arms around her. She shook slightly and pulled away before she buried her head in his chest. *Come here.*

"Did you feel that?" asked Maggie.

Yes. This feels right.

"No, did you feel the *hold her*?" she asked.

I thought it.

"But did you feel it?" she pressed.

I did. It felt . . . it felt right.

"That was a prompting!" Maggie shouted. "And you followed it! Hallelujah!"

That's a prompting? It's what I wanted to do anyway.

"Sometimes they are the same," explained Maggie. "But the important thing is that you followed your prompting." *It just felt right.*

Lindsey sobbed like a child and Eric held her tight. *Let me take care of you. Let me love you. It will be okay. I'm here.* After several minutes she pulled away and wiped at the tears on her face. She looked up at Eric with a sheepish smile.

"I'm sorry," she said. "I needed that." *Don't be.*

"You don't need to apologize," said Eric. *I'm here for you.* "You will never need to apologize to me." *Ever.*

"Never?" she said. "You may not always feel like that." *Try me.*

"I look forward to us finding that out," he replied. "Together."

Lindsey smiled and his heart beat rapidly. Another gust of cold wind swept down the street and blew Lindsey's hair in her face. Eric felt the cold cut right through his jacket and he saw her shiver. He took off his jacket and threw it over her shoulders. *Gentlemanly.*

"Come on, let's get you home." He put his arm around her and led her up her street.

"Well done, Eric," said Maggie. "Well done."

Thanks, Maggie. Now can you at least let me pretend it's just the two of us? Third wheel.

"Of course," she replied. "As you wish."

Friends like These

I still can't believe you got fired," Dave said.

"I didn't get fired, I quit," argued Eric. *With style.*

"Honestly, you were fired whether you quit or not," said Maggie.

Whose side are you on?

"You punched a guy out. You are lucky they didn't arrest you." Dave bent down and opened the oven. He reached inside with a pair of matching Yoda oven mitts and pulled out a muffin tin. The smell exploded into the kitchen through the open oven door.

That smells incredible, thought Maggie.

Dave placed the tin on top of the stove, closed the oven door, and removed the mitts. He plucked a steaming hot muffin from the pan and bobbled it back and forth between his hands before he tossed it over the counter to Eric. *Catch it.* Eric reached out and grabbed the muffin out of the air with his right hand. Maggie felt a searing pain that radiated from the muffin to his palm. *Ow!* Eric dropped the muffin and the melted chocolate chips smeared into the counter. *Holy geez!*

"Dang it, Dave," he shouted. "What is your deal?" *Lunatic. That was hot.*

Dave paid no attention to his complaints but stared blankly into the open refrigerator. "We're out of milk," he stated to the room. *We? I'm out of milk. There's no we.*

"Well you are welcome to go buy some," said Eric. *You can replace the eggs, flour, and chocolate chips you used while you're at it.*

"Nah, that's okay," Dave said as he closed the refrigerator door. "It can wait till you get to the store next." *Of course it can. Hobo. Mooch.*

Eric wiped at the chocolate smears on the counter and removed the muffin from the paper wrapper. Dave snatched another muffin from the tin and bounced it around in his hands while he blew frantically on it. *Let it cool. Impatient.* He made his way around the corner and sat on the stool next to where Eric stood. After he too carefully excavated his muffin from the wrapper, Dave broke off a piece from the top and blew on it. *The top is the best. Save the best for last.* Eric twisted the bottom of his muffin off and gently laid the top back on the unfolded wrapper.

"So what are you going to do now?" Dave asked with a mouthful of hot muffin. *For starters I'll chew with my mouth closed.*

"My only immediate plans involve changing my locks and hiding the baking powder," Eric quipped. *Good one. Man, you are clever.*

"Beware of pride, Eric," said Maggie.

And there's my built-in killjoy.

"I am only looking out for you," replied Maggie.

I don't need you to look out for me. I need you to find your way back to the blu bliti blah nebula, or wherever you came from.

"Ha ha," replied Dave. "Most people would be grateful for someone who got up early and made them chocolate chip muffins in the morning." *Most people wouldn't have had that someone sneak into their house and use their oven and their food to make said muffins though.*

"You could be grateful for his kindness just the same," said Maggie.

Kindness? He'd starve without me. He should be grateful for me.

"I believe he is," she replied. "Perhaps the muffins are his way of showing it."

Crud, she's right. I hate that.

Eric took a big bite of the bottom half of his muffin. As he chewed Maggie felt as if a symphony of flavor played in his mouth. She savored the textures and tastes that swirled together.

That is better than toast, she thought.

"You're right," said Eric. "Thank you, Dave. These muffins are delicious." *He can bake that's for sure.*

"You are welcome," said Dave. "And thank you for the use of your kitchen." *And my food.*

"You're welcome," he replied.

"There. Does that not feel better?" asked Maggie.

You never stop, do you?

Eric and Dave continued to chew in silence for a few minutes until their muffins had been completely consumed. Dave began to pick at the whiskers in his beard. He looked down at his fingers and quickly licked the chocolate off of them. *Gross. Beard goo.*

"Seriously, though," Dave began. "What's your plan?" *Date.*

"I honestly haven't thought much past tonight," he replied. *Lindsey. Bright Eyes. Love.*

"Ah yes, the second date with the Lindsey." Dave nudged Eric with his elbow and winked. *Don't call her "the Lindsey." It's Lindsey, just Lindsey.* "What are you two love birds gonna do?"

Obnoxious. "I don't know really," Eric replied. "I was thinking something low key. Maybe dinner and some Fro Yo, possibly a movie." *Don't say Fro Yo, you sound like a tool. Star Wars.*

"As long as it's not Star Wars," Dave warned. *Mind reader. Witchcraft.*

"I wasn't going to watch Star Wars," said Eric. *Yes I was.* "But what's wrong with it?"

"Nothing is wrong with Star Wars," replied Dave. "I'm not sure a grown man's obsession with it is exactly what a girl is looking for in a long-term relationship." *He's got a point. Probably should spring for a movie ticket anyway. New release?*

"Well I wasn't planning on watching Star Wars," he said. "I was thinking of *The Theory of Everything.*" *Girls like biopics, right?*

"What is that?" asked Dave. *Oh right, he hasn't got a TV.*

"It's that movie about Stephen Hawking." Eric pushed back from the counter where he leaned and walked into the kitchen. He dropped his muffin wrapper into the trash can and surveyed the muffins on the stove.

"The physicist?" exclaimed Dave. "You're such a nerd." *Whatever. You don't know.*

"Whatever, man," Eric argued. "It looks like a love story." *I hope. I have no idea what she likes. What kind of movies would a girl like her enjoy?*

"She probably would prefer to not see a movie at all," Maggie interjected.

Good point.

Dave joined Eric in the kitchen and they both selected a second muffin from the pan. This time Maggie only felt a slight warming sensation as Eric patted the pastry back and forth in his hands. *Best for last.* Eric methodically removed the muffin from the paper while Dave took a bite from the top of the muffin. *Barbarian. I think he just ate some of the wrapper.*

"What are you going to do between now and then?" Dave asked as crumbs flew from his mouth, into his beard. *Gross. Close your mouth.* A tiny morsel landed on Eric's chin. *Ah! Disease.* He quickly wiped it off and stepped back to a safe distance by the pantry.

"I don't know," he replied. "I should probably look for a job." *Unemployed.*

"There you go," Dave said throwing his hands up in the air. "Just what they want you to do. Emancipate yourself from mental slavery. None but ourselves can free our mind." *What is he talking about? Is that Bob Marley?*

"You want me to go live in the park with you?" Eric asked. *Homeless.*

"I don't live in the park," replied Dave. "I am an adventurer. I live where I like. When time comes for sleep I lay my weary head where I choose. I am beholden to no one." *Beholden.*

Maggie wondered who Dave's curator was and what adventures they had witnessed. She thought of Dae back at DOTAR and what must have transpired since her leap. What did she think of all this and what had been spoken of her? She thought of Borador still waiting for his turn.

My turn, she thought. It was forfeit now. All of the hopes she had for her time had been abandoned the moment she leapt through that portal. And now she was stuck there with her beholden. There was no taking back what she had done, no undoing of the events that had unfolded since. She was a leaper now and would have to face the consequences of her decision.

"Maggie." The words escaped his lips without him even realizing it.

"Who's Maggie?" asked Dave. *Shoot.*

"Uh, what?" stammered Eric. *Think of something quick.*

"You just said Maggie," Dave replied as he tossed his second muffin wrapper in the trash. *Think.* "Who is Maggie?" *Lie.*

"Do not lie, Eric," Maggie protested.

You want me to tell him that a girl from outer space is living inside my head and tells me what to do? That's crazy even by Dave standards.

"Well I would not say it like that," she replied.

Eric put down his half eaten muffin and placed his hands over his face. *Ah. Here we go.*

"It's kind of difficult to explain," he spoke with his fingers and hands covering his mouth and nose. *Start from the beginning. No explain first. Explain what? Ack!*

"I'm listening," Dave said as he leaned in and his eyes widened slightly. *Well you've got to tell him now. Have him sit down first.*

"You'd better sit down for this." Eric led the way into the living room and they each took their place on opposite ends of the futon. Dave turned sideways and sat cross-legged with his hands in his lap while Eric leaned against the arm of the futon and looked at the floor. *He's going to think you have lost your mind. Maybe he won't. Are we still sure you haven't?*

"Have faith, Eric," said Maggie. "He is your friend."

Faith. Friend. All right.

"Maggie is a . . ." he began. *Girl. Spirit. Voice.* "She's a-a voice inside my head."

Eric pointed to the side of his head. Dave's eyes widened further and glanced at the door behind him. *That didn't sound good. You are losing him. Get on with it. There's no turning back now. Just tell him.*

"She's not just a voice, she's like a person," he continued. "She came from a bureau or something that hears and records all of our thoughts and stuff. She was assigned to watch me and came here to help me." *This sounded way better inside my head.*

"And by here you mean inside your mind," questioned Dave.

"Sort of," replied Eric. "I mean she's like with me. She sees what I do and hears what I do. She even feels cold or tastes what I eat. She won't shut up about food. She's like a passenger inside my body." *Just call the guys in white coats already.*

"What does she tell you to do?" asked Dave. *What doesn't she tell me to do?*

"Good stuff," Eric assured. "She told me to help Lindsey and she tells me not to lie or think unkind thoughts, that sort of thing."

"So she's like your conscience," said Dave. *Kind of. Only more annoying.*

"I can hear you, remember?" said Maggie.

You won't let me forget.

"Not really," Eric replied. "She's not a part of me. She is a totally different spirit or something."

"Like an angel?" asked Dave. *Yes, like an angel.*

"I told you, Eric, I am not an angel," said Maggie.

Different department, yes I know. Give me a break. He'll understand the angel thing.

"Exactly," said Eric. "She's like an angel." *An angel who won't leave me alone.*

"Cool," replied Dave. *You think so?*

"Yeah?" Eric queried. *He's not freaking out. Good.* "You don't think I'm crazy?"

"Well I'm probably not the best person to judge that," Dave said. *True.* "But there is a larger universe around us than we could ever see and there are things and people tapped into that universe. If you've found something that's plugged in then you should listen." *Sounds sensible.*

"I have always liked Dave," said Maggie.

You would.

"She likes you," Eric offered. *To be fair she likes everyone.*

"Well then you should definitely listen to her then," Dave winked. *These are my advisors, an intentionally homeless freeloader and a voice in my head. How did this happen?* "So you said she can hear thoughts?" *Yes, all of them.*

"Actually I can only hear your thoughts," corrected Maggie.

"Yes, but apparently only my thoughts," Eric replied. *Not incredibly helpful.*

"Can she, like, see the future?" asked Dave. *That would be amazing, but no.*

"No," said Maggie. "I cannot see the future. That has yet to be written."

Makes sense.

"She says no," Eric replied.

What all can you do?

"I can remind you of what you have forgotten," she replied.

Lamest super power ever.

"And what does she think of your new girlfriend?" Dave asked. *Bright Eyes.*

"It's actually why she's here," explained Eric. "I missed a message or premonition . . ."

"Prompting," Maggie interrupted.

Whatever.

"So she came here so that I would help her," he continued. *She saved her.*

"Lindsey must be important then for the universe to send her," Dave replied. *Yeah.*

"The universe did not send me, Eric," said Maggie. "I chose to come. But yes, I believe Lindsey is important. All of His children are." *God's children.*

"She says that it wasn't the universe that sent her," said Eric. "Dave, do you believe in God?" *This should be interesting.*

"Oh yeah," Dave said. "Totally, there's no question. You?" *I guess so.*

"I don't know," he began. "I used to and then I didn't but now . . . I think I do. I mean, if Maggie really is here with me then she came from somewhere. That somewhere could be heaven and if there's a heaven then there's a God, right?"

There is a God in heaven.

"Did you feel that?" asked Maggie.

I did. I felt it.

"Yeah," Dave said. "Sounds good to me." *Me too.*

"Yeah." Eric nodded. "There is a God."

There is.

"So you and God's little angel have a date with a V.I.P.," Dave said. "We'd better get you ready then." *I thought I was ready.*

"What do you mean?" asked Eric. *We have like eight hours.*

"Well, for starters, you go shower and shave," replied Dave. "I'll go see if I can find a suitable shirt to iron." *Iron?*

"I don't own a dress shirt," Eric said. "Or an iron." *I keep it casual.*

"Well then," said Dave. "We've got some shopping to do." *Shopping?*

"Oh hurray," said Maggie. "That sounds like fun."

Of course it does. What could be more fun than shopping with Dude Lebowski and Jiminy Cricket?

Second Time's the Charm

Does she like this place? She hasn't said much. She's not really eating. Why did we come here? Stupid, stupid, stupid. Say something. Make her smile. This is the worst. Save this. Make a joke. Say something charming. Eric took a bite of his burger. *Does she even like burgers? Ask her. Don't ask her.*

"Do you like hamburgers?" *Ah! What are you doing?*

"Yeah." Lindsey raised her napkin to cover her mouth while she answered. *Let her finish chewing. Silence is okay.*

"This is the best open fire burger around," he continued. *What happened to silence?*

"It's really good," Lindsey answered as she took a drink of water. *Water.*

"You could have gotten a drink you know," said Eric. "You didn't have to get just water."

"I like water," she replied. *There's nothing wrong with water. Now you made it weird.*

"Calm down, Eric," Maggie interjected. "Just relax."

You relax, I'm on a date. No one relaxes on a date. Dating is like a game of playground dodgeball. You pray you'll get picked and spend the rest of the time trying not to get hit in the face. It's a nightmare but the only thing worse is not getting to play at all.

"Eric, you are being ridiculous," said Maggie. *You're ridiculous.*

"Am I?" asked Eric.

"What was that?" asked Lindsey. *O-M-GGGGGGG! I'm going to die! Why me?!*

"Nothing, I was just thinking out loud," he replied. *Nice save.*

"Yes, well done," said Maggie. "And it was true as well."

Don't patronize me; this is all your fault.

"I would love to know what you were thinking," Lindsey said. *Same to you.*

"I was wondering if you are enjoying yourself," he replied. *Don't say that! You seem insecure. You are insecure, you fraud.*

"I am," she said. "This place is, um, nice." *It's a dive.*

She looked from side to side and Eric followed her gaze. It was a shabby little eating area with less than a dozen mismatched booths and tables. Thick wood columns framed the plaster white walls. There were scores of baseball caps in a variety of styles, sizes, colors, and designs that adorned the pillars from one end of the room to the other. Behind the counter was a large grill that glowed red from the hot embers of the wood pit beneath it. Maggie had not experienced a smell comparable to the musty aroma that permeated the restaurant. She wondered if there was an aroma in the world that matched it. Every table was occupied with people as varied as the hats on the walls. An elderly couple sat in the booth closest them with a family of six at the table behind them. There was an occasional shout or discontented squeal from the smallest member of the young family but other than that there was just the low hum of conversational chatter from the multitude around them.

"How about you?" He leaned forward and rested his elbows on the table with a big smile. "What are you thinking?" *Please let it be something we can talk about.*

"I was wondering what this place was originally," she stated with another long look around the room. *Hardware store.*

"I think it was a hardware store, like Luke's," he said. *Why did you say like Luke's? Maybe she won't get the reference.*

"Luke's?" she asked with a giggle. "Like *Gilmore Girls*?" *She got the reference. This could go either way. Still, I love that she got the reference.*

"Yeah," Eric said with a sideways grin. *Just forfeited my man card but if she digs it it's totally worth it.* "Do you like *Gilmore Girls*?" *Moment of truth.*

"I was obsessed with it in high school," she said. *Me too. Don't say that.*

"Me too." *Ah! Why did you admit that?*

She brushed a strand of hair from her face and sat back in her chair with a satisfied grin. *She is so pretty. I could look at her all day long. She is kind and sweet. She'll eat tacos and burgers with me without complaint and she loves* Gilmore Girls. *If she will watch Star Wars with me and she even likes it a little, I'm marrying this girl.*

"Are you team Dean, team Jess, or team Logan?" she asked. *Easy.*

"Team Logan, totally," Eric said. "I hate Dean."

Lindsey grimaced and looked down at the table. *Uh oh.*

"Sorry," he said. "It's hard to break the habit. I didn't mean hate." *Yes I did. I hate that guy. He's a whiny jealous jerk.* "I meant I dislike his nature, his ridiculous floppy hair and everything about him."

The grimace disappeared as a laugh exploded from her lips. *Yatzhee. Nice save again.*

"His hair is ridiculous," she said. "But I'm still Team Dean." *Boo.*

"Well I'm going to have to convert you to Team Logan," Eric replied. *Or even Jess, anything but Dean.*

"That will take some serious convincing," she joked. *I'm game.* Gilmore Girls *marathon.*

"I've got time," he said. *Bright Eyes. That smile. You're staring, Eric. Stop staring.*

He looked down at the greasy remnants of his burger basket. *All gone. Delicious.*

"That was quite good," said Maggie. "It was the most enjoyable thing we have tasted thus far."

It's weird when you say things like that, it reminds me that you are inside of me.

"Since we've established your poor taste in men, what's your favorite food?" asked Eric.

Lindsey frowned and the gleam left her eyes. *Oh no. I didn't mean that.* With a faraway gaze she appeared to stare right through Eric. *Way to go funny man, you blew it.*

"I didn't mean, uh, I . . ." Eric stalled. *I can't win.*

"No, I know," said Lindsey. "It's okay." *It's not okay. Think before you speak, Eric.*

She rested her hands on the table and looked down at her burger while Eric shifted in his chair. *Tell her you don't care about her past. Tell her it's okay. Tell her how you feel.*

"Lindsey," Eric reached across the table and placed his hand gently on top of hers. She flinched but did not recoil. Her eyes met his and they stared at one another. *Those eyes.* Maggie felt a swelling in his chest and an energy emanating from their touch. "I'm sorry. It was a poor attempt at humor." *Forgive me.*

"It's fine," she said. "Really it is." *Hug her. Maybe not the right moment.*

She glanced over her shoulder toward the front door. Eric looked up at the row of hats above her head and then over to the front door as well. *Does she want to leave? Is she done eating?*

"Pizza," she said. *Huh?* "I love pizza." *Oh, favorite food. Me too.*

"Me too!" Eric exclaimed. *Too much. Calm down, you're shouting.* "Have you tried Ciro's? It's the best." *The best.*

"No I haven't." *Boom. Next time.*

"Well that's where we're going next," he declared. "You'll love it."

"Next, huh?" she responded with a tiny smirk. *Presumptuous.*

"Well, yeah," he replied. "I'm just going to keep planning our future together until you tell me to stop." *Whoa. Let's see how she takes that.*

"And what have you planned for us after this?" she asked. *Dessert. Be mysterious, girls like that. I think girls like that. I'm clueless.*

"Come on and I'll show you." Eric stood up from the table and extended a hand toward her. She wiped her hands with a napkin and discarded it atop the table. They clasped hands and he gently guided her to her feet. *Be a gentleman, get her jacket.* He removed her jacket from the back of the chair and held it up like a matador. She smiled and slipped her arms into the sleeves. *Smooth. Casanova. You got this.* He led her through the mismatched tables and chairs to the front door. As he pushed open the door a blast of cold air swept into the restaurant from the street. *Brrrr. Chilly.* They stepped out onto the sidewalk and began to walk up the street toward a bright orange and green neon sign that read Lyman's. Next to the sign was a bright white fluorescent light, shaped like an ice cream cone. Eric walked over and stood triumphantly beside the store's front window. *Ta da!*

"Are we getting ice cream?" Lindsey asked. "It's like forty degrees out." *Newbie.*

"Yes it is and Lyman's has the best hot chocolate in town," explained Eric. *The best.*

"Better than Dave's?" she asked with a bright smile. *I love this girl.*

"Way better," he replied. "I was thinking we could grab some hot chocolate and go for a walk along the river." *That's romantic, right?*

She nodded and Eric pulled open the door with a grand gesture for her to step inside. Two teenage girls manned the counter with a third girl wiping down tables against the opposite wall. Other than that, the establishment appeared to be empty. Eric followed Lindsey to the counter and watched her as she silently looked over the white board menu. *Heavenly. I could watch her all night.*

"Hold up," said the girl behind the counter. "Don't move." *What? Why?*

Startled, Eric looked up at the teenager. *What's her deal?* She had bright blue eyes and long straight red hair that framed her face like curtains. She held both hands straight up in the air and smiled broadly. *What is the matter?*

"Hey, Shay," the red-haired girl called over her shoulder.

"Yeah, Kay," replied an athletic looking blonde at the far end of the counter. *Shay? Kay?*

"I'm getting the vibe," Kay replied. *What vibe? What's happening?*

The girl wiping the tables dropped her rag and made her way over to the counter next to her blue-eyed coworkers. The three of them smiled brightly at Eric and Lindsey.

"Ooh, she's got like a radar for this," said the third girl. They all wore matching pastel orange polo shirts with teal green name tags. *Shay, Kay, and JJ?* Eric looked from one girl to the next as he read their badges. *Is this some kind of cult? Does your name have to rhyme to work here? Where's May and Ray?*

"A radar for what?" he asked. *For awkward customer greetings?*

"She can tell how many dates you've been on," replied JJ. *Bull.*

"Every time," added Shay. *All right, prove it.*

"Yep," replied Kay. "Every time."

"Okay, let's see it." Eric reached over and took Lindsey by the hand. *I hope she plays along.* He looked over at Lindsey and gave a slight nod and a wink. She nodded back and stepped closer to him. *She's game. That a girl. I love this.*

"Yes," said Lindsey. "Tell us, how many dates have we been on?"

They stood arm and arm while the red-headed young woman scrutinized them. She tilted her head to the side, put a finger to her lips and peered through squinted blue eyes at the couple. *No way she pegs this. She's got nothing.*

"Second date," Kay finally declared with a flippant finger point. *Holy cow. How in the world?*

Eric looked over at Lindsey with his mouth agape. *Unbelievable.* She returned his gaze with her own look of astonishment.

"I'm right, aren't I?" asked Kay. *No way.*

"She's right," Shay proclaimed when words failed their awe-struck customers.

"How did you know that?" asked Eric. *Mind reader. Witchcraft.*

"She's got, like, a sixth sense," replied JJ. *I see date people.*

"That is remarkable," replied Lindsey.

The three girls bumped their fists together and exchanged satisfied looks with each other.

"Well then, what are we going to order?" questioned Eric. *That's probably apparent. It's forty degrees outside and their only options are ice cream or hot chocolate.*

"Hot chocolate, of course," replied Kay. *I should order ice cream to spite her.*

"All right, we'll have two hot chocolates," Eric reached into his back pocket for his wallet. Lindsey stepped away to give him room. *Holding hands was nice. I wish it didn't have to end.* JJ joined Shay behind the counter as they prepared two cups of hot chocolate and Kay rang up the sale on the register.

"By the way, nice try with the hand holding," said Kay. "You two are precious." *We really are.*

Eric paid for the hot chocolate and the girls handed the steaming hot cups over the counter.

"Thank you very much," Lindsey said. *She is so polite. I love that.*

"Have fun," Shay called as Eric held the door open for Lindsey. *Here's hoping.*

"I really like those girls," Maggie said.

Of course you do. You like everyone.

"Yes I do," replied Maggie.

Okay hush, I need to focus on Lindsey.

"All right," Maggie agreed.

Thank you.

"You are welcome," Maggie replied.

This is not hushing.

"Sorry," said Maggie.

Okay seriously. You don't have to reply. I got it.

Eric and Lindsey left the orange and green neon lights behind them and headed up the street toward the river. The cup warmed

Eric's hand and the steam rose up to touch his rosy frozen cheeks. *The hot chocolate was genius. Good call.* The moonlight reflected off the black waters of the American River. They turned and strode down a well-lit deserted walkway accompanied only by the chirping of various insects. *Such a beautiful night. Nowhere else I'd rather be.* Lindsey carefully sipped her hot chocolate.

"How is it?" asked Eric. *Oh I hope she likes it.*

"It's good," she replied with a nod of her head. *It is good. Sweet, she likes it.*

Eric took a sip from his cup and flinched as the hot liquid touched his tongue. *Ow.* He rubbed his tongue back and forth across the roof of his mouth. *There go my taste buds.*

Maggie wondered why anyone would subject themselves to such pain and discomfort.

"So I don't really know much about your story," Lindsey said. "Tell me about your family."

"There's not much to tell," Eric began. "Only child. Folks are from back East. I don't really see my cousins or aunts and uncles, except for weddings and funerals. It's really just me and my parents." *Quiet childhood. Lonely.*

"Are you and your parents close?" she asked. *Kind of.*

"Yeah, I guess," he replied. "They are both nurses actually. That's how they met. So they have crazy schedules. When they're not working they like to read mostly. They do enjoy traveling so sometimes I don't even know where they are from week to week. But they check up on me to make sure I'm still alive and ask when I'm going to settle down. You know, parent stuff."

Lindsey frowned and looked away toward the dark river. *Shoot. I forgot her dad is the worst. This is not the topic you're looking for. Move along.*

"My dad would love you," he continued. "He likes poetry. He actually considers himself a bit of a poet. He's had a couple of them published, I think."

"Oh yeah?" her fallen expression rose slightly. *That's the ticket. Poetry. I got nothing.* "Anything I would have read?" *Not likely.*

"I don't know," he replied. "I never really took an interest, much to his disappointment."

She looked away again over the flowing tranquil waters. *Now she's disappointed. You are better than that, Eric. Think.*

"I do remember one of his poems though," offered Eric. *Or most of it anyway.*

"I'd love to hear it," answered Lindsey. *Thought you might. How does it start again?*

"Let's see," he stalled. *Light. Eyes. Skies. Bright Eyes.* "A light carries 'cross the tranquil blue; and draws me ever nearer to you. A precious jewel amid heavenly skies; leaves me helpless and lost within your eyes." *Nailed it.*

"That's beautiful," she beamed back at him. *She loves it. Well done. Thanks, Dad.*

"You know I never understood it," Eric said. "Not until I met you." *Bright Eyes.*

"Eric," sighed Lindsey.

"Save it," Eric interrupted. "This is the part where you tell me you're broken and no good for me or that I don't know you. I don't care about any of that. I like you, Lindsey. I think I love you. I want to be with you. You make me happy and I want to make you happy. There's nothing in your past that will change that. All I care about is right now and the girl that is standing here next to me." *Whoa. That just happened. Let it sink in. I hope she doesn't run.*

"Very well said, Eric," affirmed Maggie.

Thank you.

"Eric, that's not what I was going to say." Lindsey folded her arms and looked down at the ground. *Oh shoot. Way to misread that one, Nostradamus. Be patient. Let her talk.* They stopped by the bank of the lonely river. Lindsey glanced over her shoulder at the water and Eric followed her gaze out into the darkness.

"This is where I was coming," she continued without looking back at him. *Where? Here? When? Patience. Listen.* "When I got fired, I was coming here to the river. I was going to kill myself." *Holy geez.*

She choked up and tears pooled beneath her bright blue eyes. *Hold her.* Eric stepped toward her as she wiped the tears from her face. She turned and looked up at him. *Hold her. Comfort her. Tell her it will be okay. No, just listen.*

"You saved me," she went on. "You found me and you saved me. I couldn't think of a thing worth living for and then there you were, a nice guy standing out in the rain like an idiot because he cared about me." *Wow. I saved her. No, I didn't. You did, Maggie, you saved her.*

"That's why she came," Eric whispered as he stared right through Lindsey.

"What?" asked Lindsey. *Tell her.*

"That's why I came," he replied. "I came because I care about you. But you saved me first. Before you came I was miserable. I didn't care about anything anymore. You brought me out of the darkness. Lindsey, you saved me first." *Hold her.*

Eric reached down and gently took her by the arms. He stepped close to her and looked into her tear filled face. *Wipe away her tears.* With his thumb he wiped a single stream from her cheek and cradled her head in his hands. She smiled up at him. *Oh that smile. Kiss her.* He leaned in slowly and closed his eyes.

Maggie felt an irresistible force pulling at her. A bright light crept in from all sides and engulfed her. She no longer felt the confinement and shelter of Eric's tabernacle of flesh. She was being pulled through a vast expanse away from her beholden.

"Eric," Maggie said.

Consequences

Eric," Maggie called out.

"Oh, Maggie," Dae cried.

Dae and Lorn were behind the oval platform. No streams pulsed through the four white dormant walls of the box. Maggie turned her attention to where the portal should have been and saw only a blank wall. All the wonders of the physical world had vanished along with her window to it. She felt both liberated and untethered all at once. Her relief at being back where she belonged was couched by the uneasy feeling of being on her own. She could no longer feel her connection with Eric and struggled to acclimate herself to this new reality. She turned her attention to the unwelcome committee behind her old platform.

"What happened?" Maggie asked. "Where is Eric?"

"Eric has been reassigned," Lorn said. "You need to come with me."

"Is he okay?" she asked.

"Please, Maggie," Lorn replied. "I need you to come with me."

Although his tone was gentle, the urgency in his voice startled her. Maggie moved around the platform and the wall opposite the portal opened up. Dae wore a worried expression on her once bright young face. Lorn moved between Maggie and the new opening in the wall.

"We will move swiftly. Stay close and say nothing," Lorn warned.

Lorn moved through the opening and into the hall. Dae and Maggie followed tentatively. The hall on both sides was lined with spirits, all intently watching the trio who had emerged from the box. The atmosphere was unusually subdued for the busy department and their faces showed a foreboding solemnity. At no time had Maggie known such attention and her whole being desired to escape it as quickly as possible.

"Say nothing," Lorn repeated before sailing through the gauntlet.

Maggie and Dae obediently followed in silence. As they turned the corner to head toward the regulet Maggie saw Borador among the crowd. His countenance was grim and he looked as downtrodden as the day Vila disappeared beyond the veil. Maggie forced a smile and acknowledged him. He replied with a forced smile of his own and they gazed upon one another until he was a tiny dot in the distant crowd. Although the walls of the hallway pulsed with activity, as the thoughts poured in from their respective boxes, they were met with a similarly solemn assembly in the regulet, like the one they had encountered in the halls behind them. Questions swirled through Maggie's mind but she dared not utter them.

Beyond the regulet they entered a corner of the department Maggie had never before seen. There was a familiar oval platform identical to those in the box. As Lorn approached the platform it lit up and a portal opened on the wall that displayed two stone pillars and a sweeping green and gray landscape beyond, full of mountains and trees. On the distant horizon was a glorious sky that was a brilliant orange and yellow.

"Please," Lorn said with a gesture toward the portal. "Maggie, you first. Then you."

A wide-eyed Dae looked from the portal to Maggie. Lorn gave a reassuring nod to the nervous pair. Without hesitation Maggie moved forward and pressed upon the portal. She felt a familiar pull and in an instant she found herself in the center of a grand foyer peering out at the majestic view. In short order, Dae and Lorn were by her side as they all looked in awe at the world beyond the pillars. A beautiful, brightly colored creature flew through the sky above the distant mountaintops. Maggie watched its flight until Lorn drifted forward into her field of vision and drew her attention back to her situation.

"Lorn," Maggie finally said. "Did you pull me back?"

"I did not," replied Lorn. "He did."

A glorious figure walked up the stone steps toward them. He was not transparent like the trio in the foyer. He wore a brilliant white robe that flowed back behind him. His glory was brighter than the orange and yellow sunrise on the horizon and when He passed the pillars and entered the small foyer it was completely filled with light. Lorn, Dae, and Maggie bowed before Him.

"Master," Lorn greeted Him.

Maggie was filled with light and love that completely dispelled the uncertainty which had pervaded her thoughts on their journey from the box. He smiled down on them and they back at Him.

"Come," He beckoned to Lorn.

Lorn rose and moved away from Maggie and Dae until he was directly in front of Him. The beams that emanated from Him shone right through Lorn engulfing him until he was almost invisible.

"You have done well," He said. "Return to your duties and take Dae with you. You know what is to be done with her."

"Please," Maggie said. "Please do not punish Dae. This was entirely my doing. I made this choice and I alone should suffer the consequences."

He looked upon Maggie for a moment. The smile did not leave His face. He looked down at Lorn and over at Dae before he turned back to Maggie.

"Magdalena," He said in a deep but gentle voice. "We do not choose who suffers the consequences of our actions. Those consequences are affixed. But she will not be punished. Dae has been a true and loyal friend. She did not leave the post you vacated. Even while your beholden slept, she remained."

He beamed down on Dae and her countenance grew brighter as she smiled back at Him. She turned to Maggie with joy, although there was a hint of remorse in her eyes.

"Maggie, I am sorry," she said. "I tried to help. I could not think of anything else but to do what you would do. So I cataloged all of the thoughts, his and yours. I could not find a way to bring you back, so I just stayed and did what we do."

"Dae, it is I who am sorry," Maggie replied. "I should not have placed you in that position. Thank you for staying with me, for staying with Eric. I will be eternally grateful for you."

Lorn moved next to Dae and Maggie nodded to him. Her two friends sailed back through the portal and Maggie was left to face her consequences alone. She straightened herself up and awaited judgement.

"Magdalena," He began. His voice conveyed so much love that Maggie could scarcely contain it. "Tell me, what have you learned?"

"I beg your pardon," replied Maggie. "What do you mean?"

"What do you know now that you did not know before you passed through the portal?" He clarified.

She paused for a moment and reflected on her experiences.

"I learned that rain is cold and hamburgers are amazing," she said with a laugh.

He continued to study her with a smile but did not join in her laughter. Her unrequited quip caused her to reflect on Eric's undeniable influence upon her. With greater appreciation for her audience she composed herself and continued.

"I learned how hard mortality is," she continued. "You feel isolated and cut off. It is easy to feel alone even when you are surrounded by others. I learned that in that state there are those who can be cruel and indifferent towards one another, which makes life all the more difficult. I learned how desperate they feel for connection and how rare and valuable true connection is. I learned that Thou will not stop us from doing what we choose even when it is something Thou would not choose for us."

Maggie paused and glanced over His shoulder at the sky, which had turned from a brilliant orange and yellow to a bright blue. She thought of the sights and sounds, the touch and smells she had experienced through Eric. She ached as she realized she had forfeited her turn by going through the portal. Her soul mourned the loss she would suffer.

"Was your choice worth it?" He asked.

"Oh yes," Maggie replied without hesitation. "I cannot say that I do not have regrets, but if my actions prevented a tragic end to her life, or any pain, suffering, or regret for Eric, then I would choose it again regardless of what consequences I will suffer. Where you find love, you find hope, and even at this moment I am full of hope."

Tears welled up in His eyes as He beamed down on her. His countenance grew even brighter than before. Maggie wanted to both shrink from Him and throw herself into His arms all at once.

"I know what I have done," she continued. "I will accept what is to come. I have but one request of Thee. Please, will Thou tell me what will become of Eric and Lindsey? Will they be all right?"

"They are on a path that will lead each of them to great joy," He replied. "As for what is to come, that will be up to them."

"I am happy for that," said Maggie. "So what happens now?"

"That will be up to you," He replied.

"Me?" she asked. "I do not understand."

"Magdalena," he began. "You did not act out of selfishness or impatience. You did not act out of defiance or to satisfy your desires. What you did was to help another. Doing so at your own expense was noble and brave. Greater love hath none than they who sacrifice their all for their friend."

"But what I did was against Thy will," she replied. "For that I am truly sorry. As Thou hast said, the consequences are affixed."

"What you did was not against my will," He explained. "What you did was selfless. What you did was assist in the delivery of a prompting. While there are innumerable dangers to how you went about this, ones that cannot be recommended, the result in the end was in accordance with my will."

"What is it that Thou sayest?" she asked. "Am I to be allowed to finish my assignment, to return to the department?"

"No," He lovingly replied. "You cannot be permitted to return to your duties. Eric has been given to another."

"So then I will be assigned another beholden?" she asked. "I am to begin again?"

"No," He replied. "With all you have experienced, it would be unwise for you to return. I have something new in store for you. Since a sacrifice like yours has not happened before, it is right and good that your consequence should be one like none before. In time you shall have your turn and it shall be as I intended for you from the beginning. Peace be unto you. Know that I am and that I know the beginning from the end."

Maggie was nearly overcome with joy. Her turn. She would have her turn. Her countenance grew brighter and she smiled up at Him. Amid all the joy and the love one question came to her.

"In time?" asked Maggie.

"My time is not their time," He said. "You shall wait with me until your turn. Come, this shall be but a moment to thee."

Maggie's Turn

A steady rhythmic beat swelled in her ears. She heard several distant voices between the beats. There was tremendous pressure from all sides and intense pain. *Ouch.* Her dark and warm domicile had become constricting and unwelcoming. Suddenly the pressure melted away and bright light exploded into her world. She saw shadows through her swollen eyelids and the once distant voices grew closer and louder.

"Congratulations," the closest voice said. "You have a beautiful baby girl." *Who said that?*

"Whaaa," she felt her lungs swell as a high-pitched wail filled her ears. *Ah! Too bright. Too loud.*

Freed from her safe and comfortable shelter she found herself suspended in midair with a hand cradling her neck and another holding her body. *I need help.* Her eyes fluttered open and closed as she fought against the blinding light. *Hello?* Amid the flashes of dark and light she saw a figure cloaked in blue and white. Its face was covered in a shroud. *Who is that?*

"There there, little one," the soothing voice said as a hand patted her bum. "You did well."

"Can I see her?" a new softer voice called from behind her. *Mother.*

A second figure came into view and stood beside the first. He wore a black t-shirt with bright yellow lettering and had pulled his cover from his face. He had hazel eyes and light brown hair. Brown stubble covered his face except for the spot marred by a scar on his chin. *I know you. Think. You know him.* He smiled broadly at her.

"Lindsey, she's beautiful," he spoke in the direction of the soft voice. *Lindsey?*

"Let me see her," the soft voice petitioned again. *Mother.*

Her body was buffered from the cold room as she was taken into the arms of the man with hazel eyes and wrapped in a warm cloth covering. *Safe. Warm.* He pulled her close and peered down with a beaming smile. Her tiny heart swelled in her chest. *Loved.* She was carried over and placed in the bosom of a woman with long wavy blonde hair and bright blue eyes. *Mother.*

"Oh, my little angel," she said with tears in her eyes. "Look at her."

A short pudgy figure in a floral print top with a blue mouth covering began to wipe at her head and arms with a cold wet cloth. *Cold. No. Stop.*

"Whaaa! Whaaa!" she screamed again. *I do not like that.*

"She's got a set of lungs on her," said the pudgy figure. "That's good."

"Shhh," soothed the blonde haired woman with the bright blue eyes. "It's okay, baby girl."

The pudgy figure halted the onslaught with the cold cloth. *Aw. Better. Thank you.*

"Do you have a name yet?" asked the pudgy figure in the floral top. *Name.*

The blonde woman gently cradled her and swayed side to side. *That feels nice. Mother. Safe. Name.* "What do you think?" Lindsey asked the man with light brown hair.

"You know my vote," he replied and gestured to the yellow lettering on his dark t-shirt.

"Eric, for the last time, we're not naming her Leia," Lindsey replied. *Eric.*

"Fine," Eric pouted and folded his arms across his chest. *Eric. Father.*

"I like your first choice," Lindsey replied. *Choice.*

"You think?" Eric asked as he tilted his head sideways and leaned in. *Father.*

The pudgy figure returned and pulled a pink and blue striped cap over her tiny head. *Cozy.*

"I think it's fitting," replied Lindsey.

She looked up into the bright blue eyes of her mother. Warmth rushed from her head to her toes. *Joy. Safe.* Lindsey placed a hand on her chest and she grasped her mother's finger with her tiny hand. *Love. Loved.*

"Yeah," said Eric. "I'm good with that."

"Yeah?" asked Lindsey.

"Yeah." Eric replied.

"Okay," Lindsey spoke softly to her. "You have a name, Maggie." *Maggie.*

Eric leaned in and kissed her gently on her tiny forehead. "Hey'll Maggie." *Hey.*

"Hail Maggie," Lindsey added as she and Eric gazed down on their little girl. *Hail Mother.*

Epilogue

With the addition of little Maggie, Lindsey and Eric felt their lives were complete. She was loved and adored by her parents and her "Uncle" Dave. Their adoration, however, paled in comparison with that of her younger siblings. The love in their home grew with each new arrival until their little three-bedroom house nearly burst. As Maggie likes to tell it, they needed more space for all the love, so they moved the family to Salt Lake City where Eric's business partner, Stephen Harper, lived. Young Maggie had a voracious appetite for love, literature, and life. There were hardly enough hours in the day to see and learn and do all she desired. Her passion was so infectious that Lindsey decided to go back to school. She graduated with a bachelor's degree in Marriage and Family Studies the same year that Maggie left on a mission to France.

While serving in Paris she met a Chadian refugee named Atia and her young son, Tonnerre. You can imagine my joy as I saw all of my dear friends reunited again. They of course became instant friends and often joked that they must have known each other in another life. Maggie saw Atia and Tonnerre baptized before she left France and they stay in constant contact to this day. Tonnerre, Atia's Thunderer, is a man now and has a family of his own. Through all the trials and travails of their lives, he always loved and cared for his mother. Atia is an old woman now and will soon finish her mortal journey. When she does my turn will begin. I am confident there is not another curator in the department who has seen the things I have seen or has been as privileged as I have been to have witnessed so many of those I love in their mortal journey. Though my memories of these things may be veiled from me for a time, I will never forget the lessons I learned from my friend Maggie. I pray that I can be as courageous and faithful as she, and though I am not likely to see them in my lifetime, I look forward to the day when I will see my friends again.

Acknowledgments

I didn't realize how tricky acknowledgments can be until I wrote my first one. I'm still in trouble for all the people I left out. Although I don't have a symphony orchestra waiting to play me out if I go too long, like an Oscar winner, I do feel somewhat limited by who I can thank on this page and if I thank one person specifically then it cascades into the next and the next and still somehow I'll leave somebody out.

In many ways it makes me grateful to think about it. So many people have touched my life and are worthy of acknowledgment. I am very blessed to have been surrounded by so many wonderful, and in some case insane and colorful, influences in my life. You all provide such depth to these characters and richness to my stories.

However, in my efforts not to leave anybody out I'm not going to specifically name any of you but simply say thank you. Thank you for supporting me and caring about the stories I tell. Thank you for your encouragement and the time you've dedicated from your life to myself and my life. And thank you, thank you, thank you for reading this book and telling your friends and loved ones about it. It means the world to me.

Author Biography

Author of *The Land of Look Behind*, Aaron was born and raised in Arizona and is proud to call the desert home. He came of age in the suburbs of Sacramento, California, and as a missionary for The Church of Jesus Christ of Latter-day Saints in Jamaica, where he fell in love with the people and their culture. But he has always been drawn back to the valley of the sun.

He married his childhood crush (the girl of his dreams) in 2001. Together they are raising four beautiful and rambunctious children. Before becoming an author, he worked as a freelance sports reporter for *The Arizona Republic* for nearly ten years, combining his love of writing and sports. When not working, writing, or serving at church, Aaron enjoys chasing a small white ball through the forest and beaches of his local golf course.

His storytelling draws heavily from his love of pop culture, history, adventure, his faith, and his own life experiences.